The Adventure Begins
The Adventures of Silver Dove, Book One
Eliza Scalia
Cover Illustration by: Suji Gallianetti

Dedicated to
Cynthia Hickey for taking a chance
and publishing me,
Suji Gallianetti for drawing my cover,
and Ally Householder
for being the first to look over my book.

Chapter One
Colomba-
Four Years From Now

A normal life, that's what everyone calls it, yet each person's life is so different from everyone else's. There is nothing normal about anyone's life, it is as not normal as you can get. My name is Colomba and I will soon be a graduate of Drew's Hollow High School in the small town of Drew's Hollow and, to be honest, I'm surprised that I have made it this far. After all of the things that I have seen and done, I'm just shocked that I survived! Well, I still have time before I graduate; maybe my good luck will end, and I will wind up dead, who knows? I have fought so many battles, and almost always came out the victor, but this battle may be my final one, this opponent may just be too strong.

There is a lot of stuff going on right now and I might not make it out alive, but after everything I have done and learned in the past four years I know that every moment is precious, and I don't want a minute of my time to be forgotten. That's why I am writing it all down here, I can't let any of what has happened to be forgotten. I am afraid, but I won't let my fear control me, I will not run away, I will fight. I have always fought for what I believe in and I don't plan on stopping now.

Mom, if you can see me up in Heaven, I just want you to know that I have tried my best. I have failed a few times, I will admit that, but I always picked myself up and tried again. This is what I am doing now, I am picking myself back up. I have fallen hard this time and I don't know if I will recover. It may be a slight comfort to know that I may be with you someday soon. I want to see you so bad Mom, yet I don't want to die either. I love my life, but I may have to sacrifice it if I am to do the right thing. I think you would have encouraged me to always do the right thing, that is what mothers are supposed to encourage.

It's funny to know that I used to think that my life was normal, but all that changed one day, on my first day of freshman year to be exact. Man, I was a bundle of nerves that day, worried about being in a new school, worried about making new friends, and worried about being a freshman. I was so scared it was amazing that I got out of bed that morning. It all started as soon as I got on the bus.

Chapter Two
Colomba-
A Normal Life

Okay, just breathe, just breathe and everything will be fine. I keep repeating that in my head over and over again, I'm so nervous that I feel like I'm going to explode. I felt fine when I was at my house but as soon as I got on the bus my insides started freaking out. My stomach feels like it's in my throat, my heart is racing, and my hands are shaking in my nervousness. My grandma, or Nonna as I call her, had even made blueberry pancakes, my favorite, for breakfast this morning since she knew I was going to be scared.

I live with my dad and Nonna in a small house on the outskirts of town. My mom died when I was a baby, so my dad asked for my Nonna to live with us to take care of me, so that he could go to work, and she's been with us ever since. Nonna has always been like a mother to me. She once told me that she wanted to be as good of a mother as her daughter would have been to me if she was still alive. I can easily say that she has succeeded, I could never have asked for a better substitute mom. She is always there for me when I need help, she has helped me become a better person, and she has taught me many things like reading, cooking, and how to speak her original language, Italian.

Sitting alone on the bus, I finally start calming down when I see my best friend Natalie get on the bus. Natalie has been my best friend since Kindergarten and she's the best friend anybody could have. Natalie has big brown eyes that remind me of a rabbit, gentle and kind, yet also nervous and shy. Her skin is the color of coffee and her hair is always done in intricate braids that she once tried to teach me how to do, yet I couldn't get the hang of it. She is around an inch taller than me, but, since she is always slouched over, we appear to be around the same height.

Natalie sits down beside me and gives me a big hug.

"How are you, Birdy?" Birdy, the nickname she gave me when we first met. When we first introduced ourselves and I told her that my name meant Dove in Italian she just started calling me Birdy. Ever since that day, she is the only one that I allow to call me Birdy.

"I'm doing alright I guess, how are you Nat?" Nat, my nickname for her.

"I'm okay, I'm a little scared." I can tell that she's more than a little scared because she's twirling a braid of her hair around her finger, it's something she always does when she's terrified. I know that she's just as afraid as I am about starting at this new school, probably even more afraid than me. Nat has always been the shy one between the two of us while I'm more outgoing. Even though she can be very shy, she is very loyal. She will always stand up for someone that she considers to be her friend, and I'm honored to be considered her best friend.

We have been talking about this day all summer, telling each other how excited we are about starting high school. I think that we can both clearly see that we were lying. We're not excited, we're terrified! We talked on the phone for hours last night, telling each other what we want to do now that we're in high school. I want to get into a bunch of different clubs while Nat wants to come out of her shell and make more friends.

We have both been in the same private school since we were in Kindergarten, and neither of us have any experience dealing with a massive place like the public high school we are now attending. Our eighth-grade class only had thirteen people in it all together.

"Don't worry, I'm sure everything will be fine." The bus stops to let another person on. He's a tall guy who appears to be around the same age as me, although I don't recognize him at all.

His dark hair hangs in his face, covering his eyes. The guy holds his books in front of his chest like a shield from the world as his head hangs down to stare at the ground. He looks as if he isn't terrified about starting this school year like Nat and I are, he looks like he's absolutely dreading it, as if this is his first day of torture. He walks past me and doesn't even look at anyone else as he makes his way to the back of the bus to sit by himself. I don't know why but something makes me want to go back and sit by him, I don't want him to feel so lonely, I want to see him smile. I get that thought out of my head, I can't just force my friendship on him, maybe he wants to be alone.

I continue talking with Nat until the bus finally makes it to my new school. As Nat and I look through the window at our new school, I take in a deep breath and look at my best friend.

"Are you ready Nat?" She releases a deep breath.

"I hope so." We take each other's hands and we walk out of the bus together. Only a minute after we step out of the bus, the lonely boy that had been on my bus tripped over a purse that was sitting on the ground and he fell, his books and pencils tumbling out of his hands and going all over the place.

As the boy picks himself up and starts putting his stuff back into his backpack an angry voice shouts out, *"Look what you've done!"* A blonde girl picks up the leather purse that the boy had tripped over and holds it over him as he looks up at her with terror. I can understand why he's so scared, the girl standing over him is Angela Turner, the meanest girl there was in my old private school, and she's probably going to be the meanest girl in high school.

Angela stands a few inches taller than me, but since she always has her nose stuck in the air that might add an inch or two toward her height. I'm not an expert at this, but I am pretty sure that her blonde hair is fake, I can see how there is a slight change in color toward the roots of her hair. If her hair wasn't dyed I would assume that it would be a dull brown color, similar to the color of really dirty dish water. Her brown eyes are always looking down on you, even if you are taller than her. Angela's lips are always creased into a permanent scowl that makes her already foreboding presence even more unpleasant. Makeup is practically plastered all over her face, making her expressions seem a little like a plastic doll, if some toy company actually manufactures a toy that scowls at people. If she would wear less makeup and stop looking at people as if they are bugs beneath her feet, she might actually be good looking. I wouldn't know though, I have never seen her look at anybody with even the slightest hint of kindness or equality.

Her clothes show the same level of assumed superiority that she has. Skinny jeans practically strangle her thin legs while a tight-fitting white blouse shows off her thin figure. She is so thin that I'm surprised that she doesn't just blow away in the slightest breeze. I know that she takes pleasure in her tiny figure though since she would show off about it all the time during middle school and call every girl who was even slightly bigger than her fat. A pale pink leather jacket covers her shoulders but hangs open so that everyone can still see her shirt, so they can see the full extent of her daddy's wallet. With my keen eye, I can see that every single article of her attire is outrageously expensive, including the purse that Angela is now shaking in front of the poor boy's face.

"Your ugly shoes got dirt all over my new purse!" I look at the purse to see that only a few

specks of dirt are on the bag, it's barely even noticeable. The boy tries to say something to her but all that comes out is a bunch of mumbling that I can't understand even though I am only a few feet away from him. It looks like Angela is about to yell at him again, without thinking I step in between her and the boy.

"Your purse was on the ground Angela, it's understandable that he tripped over it. You don't need to yell at him." Angela seems surprised that I stood up for him, but her surprise doesn't make her stop yelling. Her brown eyes narrow and her perfectly tanned face contorts in rage.

"Don't start defending someone who ruins other people's stuff Colomba! Wait until my daddy hears about this!" Angela folds her arms in front of her chest and sticks her nose farther up in the air than it usually is. We all know who her father is; he's the principal of the school and one of the richest men in town since he is the heir to a fish cannery. Angela is the perfect picture of the mean, rich girl. Her blonde hair is always perfectly styled, and her clothes are obviously expensive. She is always primped, polished, and brushed to perfection, and she doesn't let anyone forget it.

"I'm sure that your dad will understand that this was just an accident-"

"Well what about my purse, it's ruined!" She holds the bag in front of my face, only an inch away from my nose.

"It's just a little dirt Angela, you can just brush it off, your purse is fine." Angela takes her purse out of my face and puts her hands on her hips as she glares at me.

"Well, we'll just see what my Daddy has to say about it." with that said, she turns away from me and marches through the front doors of the school. Whenever she walked past somebody they would move out of her way, afraid of getting too close. I turn away from her as well to look down at the lonely boy from the bus. He's staring up at me, his eyes wide in wonder.

"Are you alright?" I hold my hand out to him, which he accepts. I help him back up to his feet.

By standing right in front of him I can see that he is almost half a foot taller than me. His black hair hangs in his face, as if he is trying to hide himself from the world behind the curtain of his bangs. His dark eyes are the color of chocolate, a rich color full of warmth that is sadly hidden behind his shyness. His limbs are long, almost a little too long, as if he hasn't completely grown into them yet. My guess would be that, even though he is already tall, he still has more growing to do in his life. It's almost as if I am looking at a puppy whose paws are too big for the rest of his body, so he is constantly tripping over them.

"I-I'm alright." his voice is soft and gentle, but it is deep, and I can tell that there may be some power to his voice buried inside although he might be too afraid to reveal it. "Thank you so much."

"Don't worry about it, you get used to Angela, she's a bit of a pain but she can be avoided. Whenever you hear her coming, just run for the hills, it's safer that way." he actually laughs at my last remark. His laugh sounds like it isn't used that much, it seems unsure and awkward. Too bad, it's a sweet sounding laugh. I hold my hand out to him. "My name is Colomba." he takes my hand and shakes it gently, almost nervously.

"I'm Luis." a small, shy smile pulls at the corners of his lips. I smile warmly at him and he just stares at me as if he's enchanted by me. Why is he staring at me like that? Is he just grateful that I helped him out with Angela? I'm not sure what it is, but I know that he is a good person, I can see it in his eyes. I may not understand the look he is giving me, but I know that I can trust him.

"It's nice to meet you Luis, I hope I can see you in one of my classes. I'll see you later." I walk away with Nat walking beside me. Behind me I can faintly hear Luis give me an almost whispered, "Bye."

Nat and I head inside to get to our first class, one that we thankfully share. Once we are a good distance away Nat bursts out laughing.

"What's so funny?" Nat's eyes sparkle with amusement while her lips are pulled up in a childish grin.

"Someone has a crush."

"What are you talking about Nat? I don't have a crush on anybody." Nat stops laughing to look at me as if I'm being silly.

"I'm not talking about you Birdy, I'm talking about Luis. Did you see the way he was looking at you? It was so cute, love at first sight." I shake my head at her.

"Stop it Nat, he was just being grateful. I did just help him deal with Angela, anybody would be friendly after that, don't you think?" Nat shakes her head at me just like I did to her a second ago.

"Birdy, Birdy, Birdy. You can be so blind sometimes; he obviously feels something for you. Anybody who saw him looking at you could see that." I have to force myself to not roll my eyes at her. Nat has always had her mind on romance, even when we were little. She just loves love stories so much that she wants to see one in real life. Maybe she can start a relationship now that we're in high school, so she won't keep projecting these romantic fantasies on me.

"Please don't start making something out of nothing, now come on we need to get to class. We don't want to be late on our first day." I know that we still have plenty of time until our first class starts, but I just want to end that conversation, Nat could go on with that forever. I may not know much about romance but it's not something I want to focus on right now. I've just started high school, I want to work on my classes and get good grades. I want to go to a good college one day and be a doctor just like my mom. No matter what happens, I can't let myself be distracted by something I don't need, like romance, not even if my best friend wants me to.

It only takes Nat and me a minute or two to make it to our first class. As we both stand in front of the door, we look to each other and hug, knowing just how nervous we both are. Placing my hand on the doorknob, I take a deep breath and open the door, starting my first day of high school.

<u>Chapter Three</u>
Luis-
Four Years From Now

I don't know what to do, I have never been so afraid in my entire life. I'm not even really afraid for myself. I am afraid for the person I love more than anything in the world. The person who has always been there for me, who has always accepted me the way that I am even though the world has always cast me out. We are both in danger and we may not live to see our graduation from high school. We both know this and that's why I am writing this down. I suppose you could consider this to be my own biography, just in case I am never able to tell my story to the world.

I have always been invisible to everyone around me, but I don't want to be forgotten. I don't want to be invisible in death as well as life, and the only way I can do that is to write down all of the adventures that I have had since I started high school, when all of this began. People may not believe my story, but I still feel as if I need to tell it.

It all started with her, because of her, the one

person I can't live without. She was in my mind and heart in everything I did. She gave me hope when I felt like the world was going to crash in around me. There was always a smile on her face to brighten my day, even when it felt like the sun was never going to shine again. She is why I am standing my ground now. If I have to die so she can live, then I am willing to do so. After all the good she has done in this world she deserves to keep living, even if she gets to live without me. After everything I have done, I may not deserve a happily ever after, but if I die knowing that she gets to live, then I will die with a smile on my face.

As I write this now, I remember that first day I saw her, the first day of my freshman year of high school. I had been dreading the start of school, believing that I would be isolated from everyone else just like I had always been, but she changed that for me. When I first saw her, I admit that it was under strange circumstances, but I wouldn't change it for anything because it showed me just how good of a person she is. If I do die, and she reads this, I hope that she can find it in her heart to feel something back for me.

Chapter Four
Luis-
The Most Amazing Girl in the World

She's standing over me, confronting the blonde girl who had been yelling at me. Even though the blonde girl is yelling at her she's not backing down, she's standing up for me and she doesn't even know my name.

Her light brown hair hangs down past her shoulders and her sparkling light blue eyes that remind me of aquamarines, stare straight at the blonde girl without any fear. She is rather small, probably just a little over five feet tall, yet she stands up straight with confidence. She is wearing a pale blue sundress with a white cardigan that makes her look innocent and cute. Her heart-shaped face and eyes the color of the ocean reminds me of an angel. The blonde girl walks away from us in a huff and marches through the school doors, her hands clenched into fists. Only when she is out of sight does the girl standing over me look down in my eyes.

"Are you alright?" She holds out her hand to me, which I eagerly accept. As she helps me back up to my feet I try to give her my response.

"I-I'm alright." Stupid, stupid, stupid. Why did my first words to her have to come out in a stutter? She either doesn't notice this or decides to ignore it (which I am extremely grateful for). She smiles at me, making my heart race in my chest. "Thank you so much."

"Don't worry about it, you get used to Angela, she's a bit of a pain but she can be avoided. Whenever you hear her coming, just run for the hills, it's safer that way." I laugh at her words but even I can tell that it sounds a little awkward. I suppose I'm not used to laughing anymore, I haven't really had any friends to laugh with in a long time. She holds her hand out to me. "My name is Colomba." Colomba, what a beautiful name. I take her hand gently, afraid that she will feel my hand shaking and think that I am a complete dork.

"I'm Luis." I smile at her, I'm so glad that she is looking me in the face or else she would have noticed how my legs are shaking. It takes everything I have to keep myself standing on my wobbly legs. When I glance over her shoulder to look at her friend, she is smirking at me with a knowing look and I realize that I had been staring at Colomba. Embarrassment sends a block of ice down into my stomach as I look away from Colomba's friend. Dang, now her friend is going to tell her how I was staring at her like a freak as soon as they walk away.

"It's nice to meet you Luis, I hope I can see you

in one of my classes. I'll see you later." She turns away with her friend walking beside her. As she leaves me, I whisper, "Bye," so quietly that I doubt she even heard me.

She is the most amazing girl I have ever met, and I've only known her for a minute. People have always picked on me since they all think that I am different, but I've never had anybody stand up for me the way she did, she is an angel on earth. Most people just try to ignore what is happening when they see other kids bullying me, but she did the exact opposite. She defended me against my bully, Angela, and didn't back down. I hope that I have every class with her, just being able see her everyday would make me happy.

I head to my first class with a small bit of hope, she might be there. My hope is quickly shattered when I open the door to see that she isn't in the classroom. Hanging my head, I walk to the first desk I see and sit down, staring down at the desk in front of me, hoping no one will talk to me. This is a small town so most of the people in my class will probably be the same ones that I had in middle school, the ones who would always make fun of me.

I wonder how I have never met Colomba before since we both live in such a small town. Thinking hard I realize that she must have gone to that really small private school downtown. I went to the public elementary and middle school along with practically everyone else at this school, but the private school, Doyle Academy, also had elementary and middle school classes and kept their students isolated from the rest of us.

Only the very rich, or the kids smart enough to earn a scholarship, are able to go to that school. That one blonde girl who yelled at me, Angela, looked as if she could afford to go there, but Colomba does not. Colomba dresses very nicely and everything, but something about her tells me that she's not very rich, she must have gotten a scholarship to go there, she must be super smart. I wonder if she would have teased me if she had gone to my old middle school.

Almost immediately after I think that I hear the familiar voice of Alex Donner, my main bully, the one who enjoys picking on me the most.

"Well hey there Louie!" he slaps his hand on my back as if we're friends, it stings a little as he does this, but I stay quiet. "I was hoping that I would have a class or two with you, I've missed hanging out with you over the summer." I know what he means by "hanging out", he means calling me names, pulling my pants down when I'm not paying attention, or spilling stuff on me and saying it was an accident. All of the things that make you feel like a disgusting bug in the eyes of your peers. Before he can say anything else, the teacher walks into the room, Alex gives me an evil smile before he walks back to his seat and the teacher starts class.

Alex has always enjoyed picking on me because I'm quiet and shy. I also don't have any friends who will help me whenever he comes around. He also knows that I'm weaker than him, he's very athletic while I'm more of a bookish guy. I can solve a math problem ten times as fast as him, but that doesn't really help me stand up to him. Alex has always been a popular guy; he's on the football and basketball team and he's both team's best player, he's good looking, and his family has a lot of money. It's only natural that a guy like him is popular while I'm not, I just wish that I didn't have to share a class with him. I wish I never had to see him at all.

I take out my notebook and I start taking notes on what the teacher is saying while Alex is making funny faces at me, trying to distract me. He used to do that to me all the time last year, try to distract me from class, but I'm so used to it by now that I barely even notice him. I take my notes as if nothing unusual is happening. The bell rings, signaling the end of class, so I quickly pick up my bag and rush out of the room before Alex can catch up to me. He may be a good athlete, but he can't outrun me, I learned how to run from having to get away from him all the time. Fear is good motivation for running fast.

I make it to my next class, Advanced Placement English with a teacher called Ms. Justice, before anyone else has even shown up. Sitting down in the front row, I close my eyes, hoping that Alex won't walk through the door. Several people pass by my desk, but Alex is nowhere to be seen. I let out a sigh of relief when he doesn't come in the door. I feel even happier when I see someone I know, the girl who helped me earlier today, Colomba.

She looks around the room for a moment before her eyes land on me. When she sees me her whole face breaks into a beautiful smile. Her smile is the most amazing smile I have ever seen, when she smiles at you it makes you feel as if you are the only thing in the world that matters to her. Her smile sends a rush of warmth to my face and makes me feel as if all the tension has left my body, as if her smile can take away all of my stress and worry. I think it would be impossible for anyone to be unhappy after seeing her smile.

Colomba walks straight toward me, that smile still on her face. She stops only a few feet away from me. I can actually smell her perfume from here, it smells like flowers. She points at the seat beside me.

"Can I sit here?" Right now, I am the luckiest guy on the face of the Earth. What did I do to deserve something this wonderful? It must have been something truly selfless for me just to be in the presence of someone like Colomba.

"Of course, of course." she sets her bag next to the desk and sits down. As she opens up her bag to take out a notebook, I stare at her. There is no makeup on her face, but she still looks prettier than any girl I have ever seen. I stare at her eyes the longest, she has such incredible aquamarine eyes, they're so mysterious yet so friendly. I could stare at her all day, but I know that would be a little weird for anybody to do.

I was about to try and start a conversation with her, but the teacher walked in the room and started class. I feel a bit annoyed but I'm not angry. Since Colomba is in my class I get a chance to speak to her at least once every day. I have every chance in the world to talk with her, I think that this might be my best school year ever.

Chapter Five
Colomba-
My First Day

Luis and I separate in the hallway as we both head to different classes. It's a bit hard to say goodbye to him since I am leaving one of the few people that I know at this school behind and heading straight into the unknown. My third class of the day is gym, something simple, hopefully a place where I can make a friend.

Walking into the gym, I stare at the massive room in surprise, at my old school our gym was about the size of six classrooms put together, but this place is about four times the size of that. I don't think I've ever been in a room this big before. I haven't been able to travel much in my life, so I don't have a lot of experience when it comes to different places. A basketball court is in the center of the room, closed in on two sides by tall bleachers that reach up to the ceiling. On the opposite side of the room I can see two small volleyball courts and encircling the basketball and volleyball courts is a running track. This school must have some pretty impressive sports teams if they have such an amazing gym to practice in.

Following the lead of a few other girls who walk in after me, I go into the girl's locker room. I find the locker that is assigned to me and stuff my bag inside and take out my gym uniform. The uniform is pretty simple; solid black shorts and a red T-shirt with a black picture of our school mascot, the Drew's Hollow Horseman. The picture of the Horseman kind of looks like a Revolutionary War cavalry officer. The uniform screams out school pride with the picture of our mascot and it clearly showing our school colors, red and black.

As soon as I have the uniform on, I head back into the gym to meet the rest of my class. Class hasn't quite started yet and so everyone is just standing around in the middle of the basketball court, chatting casually. I stand on the outskirts of this group of students, unsure of what to do. There appears to be around forty other kids in my class and they all seem to have their own groups of friends already. Probably the same friends that they had in middle school, while I stand alone with nobody from my old school in this class. An entire minute passes by in silence and I begin to lose hope when a voice from behind says something to me.

"Hey, I don't think I've met you before." turning around I am face to face with a very handsome guy. Dark green eyes look down at me since he stands around seven or eight inches taller than me. His light brown hair hangs over his forehead yet stays out of his eyes so that I can clearly see the happiness in his gaze as he stares at me. He is very well muscled, which is shown off by his tight-fitting gym T-shirt, he is most definitely an athlete. His teeth are blindingly white, something I can easily notice due to the huge grin spread across his face.

"Are you new to town?" the boy asks me in a deep voice. I smile shyly as I shake my head at him, hope returning that I may meet a new friend in this class.

"No, I've actually lived here my entire life." he nods his head, a spark of realization igniting in his eyes.

"Oh, I see, you must have gone to that private school, what's it called?"

"Doyle Academy."

"Yeah that place. You know, if I had known that you were in that school, I would have begged my parents to send me there." I feel my cheeks growing hot and I know that I am blushing furiously. I have never been flirted with so boldly before. Most guys are a bit more subtle about it, yet this guy is completely confident, as if he doesn't believe that failure is even possible. I have no idea how to respond to something like that, thankfully the gym teacher takes care of that for me.

"Alright everyone," the gym coach, Mr. Matthews, calls out so that his voice echoes in the spacious room. "For our first day of class I'm going to let you have a choice, you can either play basketball or partner off and play some badminton." He points out the equipment and then walks off and sits down on the bleachers, completely ignoring the class while he plays around on his cell phone. Before I can even make up my mind about what I want to do, the guy turns to me with that same confident grin.

"How about you and I pair up for badminton?" Once again, I have no idea what to say. I don't know if I should say yes, but I also can't say no, he's the first person to talk to me in this class and everyone else has already formed groups and have started playing basketball or badminton.

"Sure." I practically whisper, his already large smile grows bigger when I say it and he quickly goes off and grabs us two badminton rackets and a birdie. He returns to me and we both head to an empty volleyball court.

"So, what's your name?" he asks me.

"My name is Colomba Carter."

"Hmm, Colomba, that's a strange name, but I like it." he moves a little closer to me as we walk, and I'm tempted to move away. "My name is Alex, Alex Donner." we thankfully move away from each other so that we can play on opposite sides of the net.

He takes the first serve and the birdie practically dive-bombs to my side. Somehow, I am able to hit it with my racket so that it flies back over to his side. We strike the birdie back and forth, each of us hitting it with speed and accuracy, each of us almost missing it. Alex seems surprised, as well as impressed, by my athleticism.

I have been taking martial arts since I was very young, I may not look like it, but I am actually extremely athletic and surprisingly strong for someone of my size. Just last year I celebrated my eighth year studying Aikido, I earned my second-degree black belt in Tai Kwon Do, and I just started doing a new martial art a few months ago called Wing Chun. I may be small for my age, but I am someone to be reckoned with if anybody tries to mess with me. Thankfully I have never needed to fight back against somebody, but it is nice to be prepared in case that moment arises.

While the birdie flies between us I notice that some people in the class have stopped playing their games to watch Alex and I play. They stare at the two of us in amazement as we furiously hit the birdie back and forth. The coach even stops playing on his phone to come over and watch us. After I make a particularly impressive shot that scores me a point the coach walks up to me with a pleasant smile.

"Well Miss, you are a very impressive young lady. I never thought that I would see anybody score a point on Alex here." Alex, for some reason, grimaces slightly at the couch's comment but remains silent. "Have you ever thought about joining one of our sports teams, I think you could be a star player just like Alex here." I look down, embarrassed by his offer. I'm not really interested in joining any teams right now, but I don't want to disappoint him either. He looks so excited about having me on one of his teams.

"I'll have to think about it Sir. I'm not really sure if I can add anything more to my schedule at the moment." I feel a bit bad when his face falls, but he nods his head at me, accepting my decision.

"Alright then, make sure you think hard about it. I bet you can bring our school a lot of pride with your skill no matter what team you join." He walks away after that and returns to his game on his phone while the students who had been watching Alex and I play return to their own games.

Alex smiles at me and serves the birdie as if nothing happened. As the birdie flies through the air, Alex tries to hold a conversation while taking in deep breaths from the exertion of playing against me. Well I guess you can't really call it a conversation since he has been doing almost all of the talking. Talking about how he was the star of the football and basketball teams in middle school and how he thinks he will be the best in high school too, talking about how rich his family is, and he talks about all of the things he knows that he will accomplish in high school and in life. I only get to add in a few words in between his listing of accomplishments.

I know that he is trying to show off to me since he seems interested in me, but I don't think anything will happen between us. He's just a little too conceited for my taste. He seems very nice but obsessed with himself. I hope that we can be friends though since he is so nice to me. I won't say that to him so directly since that would probably hurt his feelings, but I will try and drop a few hints to him so that he will get the point.

As gym class goes on I find myself enjoying the game I am playing with Alex. Most people try and take it easy on me with athletics since I am so small, but he is trying his hardest. Perhaps it's only because he wants to show off to me. I just don't know what to think about this guy. He comes on a little too strong, but I think that he can be a pretty good friend if he can just learn how to talk about something besides himself.

Chapter Six
Luis-
A Different First Day

When Colomba left me to go to her third period class, it felt as if the light from my day faded. I went to my third period class, getting tripped a few times from other students passing by me. I'm almost grateful that they only tried to trip me, usually people do worse. I once had someone stick a dead rat from the science lab down the back of my shirt, everyone laughed at me as I squirmed around, trying to get it away from me. I will never forget the humiliation I felt that day, it felt as if I was going to be consumed by my embarrassment. To be honest, I don't think I would have minded if I did get consumed, maybe then I wouldn't have to live with these people messing with me all the time.

I entered the classroom and sat down at the first desk I could find right in the front row. I always make sure to sit in the front row, that way the teacher might see someone picking on me and stop them. The teacher catches someone in the act only occasionally, but I can hope that these new teachers will be a little more observant. It didn't take long for the darkness around me to grow darker; the blonde girl from this morning, Angela, walked through the door and immediately noticed me.

From the hate filled glare that she gave me I could tell that she didn't get her way when she tried to get me in trouble with her dad, the principal, over what happened with her purse. She walked down the same aisle of desks as mine and, as she passed my desk, she swiped her hand out and knocked my water bottle off my desk so that it spilled all over me. I jumped out of my seat, trying to prevent most of the water from getting on me, but the front of my shirt and pants were practically soaked. Angela walked away with a wicked grin of triumph on her face as she went to the back of the classroom and sat down at the farthest desk from the teacher.

I spent the rest of the class trying to dry myself off with some tissues that the teacher had on her desk. As soon as the bell rang, signaling the end of class, I ran out of the room before Angela could get up and try to do something else to me.

Now I am heading for my fourth period, art, a class that I am actually looking forward to. I have always loved art class, writing and drawing are some of my favorite things to do. When you write or draw something, you create your own world, you can do anything you want with it, you are free in the world you create. In the world you create, it can be a kinder, better world than the real one. I sometimes wish that I could change the world like I do with my drawings and stories so that I can make it a better place, but I know that I can't. I'm just a kid, I can't do anything like that, not yet at least.

When I enter the room, a sudden calmness comes over me and I know that I have found my home within this school. It is a large room with small sculptures, paintings, and sketches scattered throughout the room. Large tables with chairs surrounding them are in the center of the room while a tall stool stands at the front of the classroom, obviously that is where the teacher will sit. I take the seat closest to where the teacher will be, eager to hear whatever they have to say.

As the other students begin filing into the classroom, I have the familiar feeling that something bad is about to happen, the hair on the back of my neck rises and my blood turns to ice in my veins. I look up at the door to the classroom and I recognize one of the faces coming in, Alex. Alex has a huge grin on his face, his last class probably went well from what I can see. I try to hide myself behind a book, but Alex sees me behind my disguise and comes over to me. He leans against my table and stares down at me superiorly.

"Hey there Louie, it's pretty great that we get to share two classes together, isn't it?" he smirks at me, knowing that I want to say no to that question, yet I remain silent like a coward. "Well Louie, you wouldn't believe the girl I have in my last class. Boy she is hot. I bet you have never seen a girl as good looking as her, she would blow your mind, and she seemed pretty impressed with me when I showed her some of my sports skills. You probably couldn't even talk to her, she wouldn't want to talk to someone as pathetic as you, she's too good for that."

If this girl has shown any kind of interest in him that shows just how dumb she is, if she's that dumb then I don't want to talk to her.

The teacher walks in and casually sits down on the stool in the front of the classroom. Alex immediately moves away from me, seeing that his time for harassing me has ended. Thankfully all of the seats near me are taken so he has to move to the opposite side of the room. The teacher smiles at all of us with a look of tranquility in his eyes.

He is a rather tall man with dark hair that hangs a little past his jawline while a short beard covers his face. He has blue eyes that sparkle beneath his hairy exterior, making him seem like a friendly, shaggy dog. He looks around at all of his students as if he can't believe that he is so lucky to be with all of us, as if every single person in the room matters to him. He hasn't even said a word yet and I already know that I like him.

"Hello there everyone," his voice is soft and gentle, kind of surprising to hear coming out of such a tall man. "My name is Mr. Sizemore and I will be teaching you all about the incredible world of art." his smile is so full of innocent pleasure that it is impossible not to smile back at him. I find myself smiling at him, forgetting everything that Alex had been saying to me earlier, as well as everything else that has been going on today with that Angela girl and all those people tripping me in the hallway. It's as if this guy has some kind of super power that makes you forget about all of the bad things that happen to you.

"Today I want you all to grab some pencils and

paper and just draw something, anything you want. It can be a person, an animal, or just something you saw one day that you thought looked cool. Don't worry about what other people will think about it, just draw what makes you happy." he stops talking and all of the students look at him, all of them rather confused. Most teachers don't do this kind of thing, most teachers just give us an assignment, they don't let us decide how to do the assignment, yet this guy is. He chuckles softly as if he understands what we are all thinking.

"All of the paper and pencils are in the back, on top of the back table, let's get started everyone we, sadly, don't have all day." with his suggestion, everyone stands up and grabs the paper and pencils he told us to get and we return to our seats.

When I am sitting back down, I stare at the blank piece of paper, unsure of what to draw. He told us to draw something that makes us happy, but I can't think of anything. In the back of my mind I think about that girl I met earlier today, Colomba. I find myself smiling just thinking about her, but I push that idea away. I can't let anyone see me drawing a picture of a girl in class, if Alex saw that he would tease me forever because of it, he would never let me forget that I have feelings.

Instead I find something else, I think about Guerrero, or warrior in Spanish, a stray cat that lives behind my uncle's shop. He has been coming to visit me for months now and I feed him some table scraps. He is a dark brown tabby with bright yellow eyes and one ear that is a bit torn around the edge, probably from a fight with another cat.

Thinking of Guerrero, I start sketching him, paying careful attention to his eyes and torn ear.

While my classmates are chatting while they barely draw, I concentrate all of my energy and focus onto my work. When I am practically finished a voice speaks behind me, "You are doing really well." I had been so engrossed in my work that I nearly leapt out of my skin when I turned around to face the teacher, Mr. Sizemore. He smiles down at me when he sees my surprise, but he thankfully doesn't tease me about it. I look down at my work and see a picture of Guerrero that is practically lifelike, although something seems to be missing that keeps him from leaping out of the page at me.

"Thanks." I mumble softly, feeling a little embarrassed by his compliment. I'm not really used to people giving me praise, most people either ignore or tease me. He scrutinizes me with a careful eye.

"You don't sound very proud of your work, is something wrong with it?" I shrug at him.

"I don't know, it just feels as if I'm forgetting something, but I can't figure out what it is." Mr. Sizemore bends over so that he can bring his face closer to the page, scanning the piece of paper with the eyes of an expert. His face lights up after a moment and he stands up straight again.

"I think I see the issue." I look down at the page excitedly, eager to fix the problem.

"What is it?"

"Your cat doesn't have whiskers." I feel like I could slap myself for forgetting something as simple as that. With a steady hand I add a few whiskers onto my picture and then hold it up so that I can examine it. It is perfect. Mr. Sizemore chuckles at me.

"That's better, now you seem proud of your work." I smile up at him.

"Yeah, I am." Mr. Sizemore examines my work, particularly around the cat's eyes.

"You have some real talent here, your name is Luis, right?" I nod my head.

"Well I look forward to see what you create in this class Luis." he walks away after that, leaving me both confused and happy. Confused that a teacher is actually giving me credit and actually seems to care about me as a person and not just someone they have to teach. I also feel joy that he is praising me for something I usually never show people for fear that they will tease me like they always do when I find something that I enjoy.

I look up to see that Alex is glaring at me venomously. It seems that he overheard what the teacher said to me and he is not happy about it. Apparently, Alex doesn't like it when someone else gets praise instead of him. I'm almost tempted to laugh at him, what a big baby. I'm tempted, but I know I can't, if I even smile at him right now I know that he will beat me up mercilessly as soon as the final bell rings and there are no teachers around. Instead, I lower my head and continue working on my sketch, pretending that he doesn't exist. This is how I can survive and still keep what little pride Mr. Sizemore gave me. I can only hope and pray that Alex doesn't do anything to me.

As soon as the bell rings and class is over, I grab

all of my stuff in one movement and rush out of the room before Alex can even stand up. Passing through the hall I am stopped by a sweet voice coming from behind me.

"Hey Luis." turning around, I am greeted by the sight of Colomba walking up to me with a perfect smile on her face.

"Hey Colomba, what's up?" she catches up to me and we start walking together.

"Not much, just finished class, I think I'm going to like it." I suddenly feel better, all of the tension from what happened with Alex earlier leaving me as soon as I hear that she is having a good day.

"What class is that?"

"Advanced American History, it sounds pretty boring, but it's actually pretty awesome. What class did you just come out of?"

"Art." she grins at me.

"Cool, I wanted to take art, but I needed to take advanced placement classes to prepare for college." wow she's dedicated to her dreams, it's only her freshman year of high school and she's already thinking about college, I'm impressed. "Did you guys work on anything?"

"Yeah, we did some sketches, I did mine of a cat that lives in my neighborhood."

"Can I see it?" I want to kick myself, why did I have to mention that to her? Naturally she was going to want to see it when I mentioned it. Now she's going to see it and think it's terrible, but she's too nice to tell me that so she's going to lie and say it's great. I know that's what's going to happen, but I don't want to say no to her. Swallowing back my apprehension, I pull out the sketch and hand it to her, afraid to see her face when she looks at it. She remains silent for a moment and I know what she's thinking, it's awful, despite what Mr. Sizemore said. I can't believe that I thought it looked good, why am I such an idiot?

"This is incredible." I lift my head to stare at her, I can see that she is telling the truth. Her eyes are open wide as she stares at the picture in wonder.

"Really?" she nods her head, not letting her eyes leave the sketch.

"It looks so real, it's amazing." she hands the paper back to me and I place it in between two pages in one of my textbooks. "How long have you been drawing?" I shrug.

"I don't know, it's just something that I do whenever I get bored." she smiles up at me.

"Well you must get bored a lot if you have become that good." I can't help but laugh at her statement. I impressed her, I actually impressed a girl that I like. I never would have imagined that a girl like her would be impressed by something as simple as a drawing.

Colomba is just so beautiful and smart that I thought that a simple drawing of a cat would be nothing to her, but I suppose that she takes pleasure in the small things of life, like a friend's drawing. Walking down the hall together, she asks me all about art and the elements of it that I am interested in. As the conversation continues all I can think about is how this morning I thought it was unlikely that I would be able to make a friend in this new school, but now I'm talking to the sweetest girl I have ever met. It's amazing how your life can change in a single day.

Chapter Seven
Colomba-
The Adventure Begins

Well my first day of school wasn't bad at all, it was a whole lot of fun; my teachers are really nice, my classes seem interesting, and I met a lot of people who could end up being my friends. Actually, today was a fantastic first day of school. I have always gone to a private school in town, Doyle Academy, so I have always been used to small classes. The thought of going to a big high school like that was a bit frightening. Now I can see that I have nothing to worry about, I will be alright.

Stepping out of the bus, I walk to my house with a smile on my face. I can see that my dad's car isn't in the driveway, so he must still be at his office. My dad is an accountant; he has many clients, so he sometimes has to stay at his office late into the night to get everything done. I'm a little sad that he isn't here to hear about my first day of high school, but I understand, work is important too. As I open the front door I am instantly greeted by a friendly voice.

"Colomba, is that you, Tesoro?" Tesoro, my

grandmother's nickname for me. It means treasure or darling, in Italian. "Can you come in here please?" Setting my backpack down on the dining room table, I head straight into the living room where I heard my Nonna's voice.

"Hi Nonna, how are you?" she smiles warmly at me as she opens up her arms for a hug, which I happily accept. My Nonna always gives the best hugs, they always make you feel so safe and warm. I've never met anyone who has a hug that could match hers.

"I'm doing great, how was your first day?" she releases me from her hug so that we can both sit on the couch, but we still hold each other's hands.

"It was wonderful, I have a lot of great classes and I met so many people today, everyone at school seems so nice, well except Angela Turner, she's still pretty awful." Nonna nods at me, she knows all about Angela from when we were both at Doyle Academy, she knows just how cruel that girl can be. "I think that this year is going to be wonderful." she smiles at me with maternal love, she seems just as happy as I am about my great first day.

"I'm glad, I knew that everything would work out for you. You're such a smart, sweet girl, it would be almost impossible for you to not make friends." my smile fades as I think about one specific person that I met today.

"Something else happened though," Nonna's smile fades as well when she sees my expression. "Right before school started a boy I met, Luis, tripped over Angela's purse and she started yelling at him." Nonna nods at this, completely understanding what I mean. She has heard many stories about people being harassed by Angela because she took something that they did as insulting to her, even if it was something so small that nobody else seemed to register it.

"What happened?" she asks in a soft voice.

"Well when she started yelling at him, I ran in between them and stood up for him, I told her that it was an accident and that she had no right to scream at him like that." Nonna smiles at me again, hugging me tightly.

"That's wonderful Tesoro, I'm so happy that you did the right thing." Her joy fades a little as she becomes more serious. "I actually have something for you, I've been thinking about giving this to you for quite a while. I was probably going to give this to you for your sixteenth birthday, or when I thought you would be responsible enough, but after what you just told me, I think you are ready for it." she reaches into the pocket of her dress and pulls out a small white box with a red ribbon on top.

"Nonna, you didn't have to get me anything." Even though I say that, I feel eager to open the box which she hands to me. I don't think anybody can be calm when they're about to open a present, it's impossible.

"I know, but this is more of a responsibility than a present." Opening the box, I find a little silver pin in the shape of a dove, its wings spread open wide in flight.

"Nonna it's beautiful." taking it out of the box, I hold it up to the light before I pin it to my cardigan. "I love it."

"I'm glad you like it, I have had it for a very long time and I was waiting for the right time to give it to you." I stare down at the pin, it is so beautiful, I love it already. "This pin is actually very special."

"Really?"

"Yes, it has special powers." I smile at her.

"No, it doesn't. You're trying to trick me, but it won't work." She smiles at me too.

"I'm not messing with you Tesoro, I promise." I still don't believe her.

"You're trying to play a prank on me, aren't you?" she shakes her head at me, the smile still on her face.

"Alright, if you don't believe me then I want you to place your hand over the pin and say, 'peaceful warrior'. That will prove that I'm telling the truth." I playfully roll my eyes at her.

"Okay then," I place my hand over the pin, not expecting anything to happen, "peaceful warrior."

All at once, the pin on my shirt starts glowing and it feels like a strong wind is blowing through the room, my heart races in panic. My hair is whipping around my face from the force of the wind, yet nothing else in the room is moving. There are a few papers sitting on the coffee table beside me, but they aren't moving at all, it's as if the wind is encircled around me. The pin starts glowing even brighter and I have to close my eyes because of it. As soon as it had started, it was over.

Opening my eyes, I see that I am no longer wearing my old clothes. I am now wearing armor like a Trojan warrior, except mine looks a bit different. My armor is silver, and the breast plate has a bird with its wings spread out over my chest while the bottom has a white pleated skirt. I can also feel a helmet on my face with a piece of metal that goes over my nose, to protect me from being hit in the face, while the helmet comes all the way down and covers the sides of my head. In my hand I am holding a sword, like what a medieval knight would use. The hilt of the sword is carved to look like a bird with its wings spread out. It is around three feet long and very heavy, it feels like it weighs twenty pounds. The end of the sword comes together into a triangular tip that is a bit intimidating since I know that something like this can be deadly in a cruel hand. When I look around at myself I almost scream, I have wings coming out of my back! The wings are nearly seven feet across and they are white and covered with feathers, they look like beautiful angel wings.

"What's going on?!" Nonna smiles at my surprise.

"I told you that the pin has special powers." Nonna now has that I-told-you-so tone that usually annoys me, but I'm too freaked out to care.

"What's going on?! Wait where are my clothes?!" I look around myself, but I can't seem to figure out where the dress I was wearing went. Nonna tries to stifle a laugh that is threatening to leave her lips as she sees my distress.

"It's alright Tesoro, your clothes will come back, I promise." I know that she's trying to comfort me, but it isn't working, my heart races in my confusion and fear.

""Come back", where did they go?!" Nonna looks away from me for a moment, a common thing she does when she doesn't know how to answer one of my questions.

"Well I'm not really sure where they went, but your clothes will come back as soon as you transform back into your regular self."

"What do you mean "transform back", what is going on with me?!" Nonna takes a deep breath before she answers my question.

"The pin you are wearing is magical. When you wear it and say the magic words, you transform into the superhero Silver Dove, the protector of peace. It's your job to defeat those who want to spread evil to the world." There are so many things that I really want to ask her, but I try to start with the most important questions.

"How did you get this pin? And how do you know about all of this stuff?" Nonna smiles, she's looking off into the distance as if she's remembering something wonderful.

"When I was around your age, I got the pin from an older woman who I had saved from a dog that was chasing her. She told me that she was the Silver Dove when she was a young woman. She explained everything to me about the pin, and then I became the next Silver Dove."

"Okay, but I'm not cut out to be a superhero, I don't have what it takes to do something like this." she wraps her arms around me in a tight hug.

"Of course, you do, Tesoro. I've watched you grow up, you are smart, kind, and strong. You can do whatever you set your mind to. Besides, ever since you were young you have been studying martial arts, you can take care of yourself. There is no reason to be afraid."

"But what if I mess up or something?" she chuckles at me, shaking her head.

"You will mess up once or twice, but that's all part of learning. Some of these mess ups will be big since you have super powers, but you will find a way to fix them. I know that you are the kind of person who won't stop until they have fixed the problem they created. You will be fine, I promise."

"Okay, but what am I supposed to do? And how am I supposed to use my powers?"

"Don't worry, I will explain everything to you."

Chapter Eight
Luis-
The Medal

Today actually wasn't that bad. I have two classes with Alex and another one with Angela, but I share three out of my seven classes with Colomba. I can't believe how lucky I am to share so many classes with her.

As I step off the bus, I walk down the sidewalk in downtown Drew's Hollow to head to my Uncle Diego's antique shop. My Uncle Diego has raised me since I was three years old when my parents died in a car accident. The three of them came to America from Puerto Rico before I was born. My mom and dad had opened a dance studio while my uncle opened his antique shop.

When I open the door to my uncle's shop, the bell above the door rings. My uncle's head appears from behind a display of old teacups when he hears the bell, his face breaks out in a large grin when he sees me.

"Hola, Tigre." Tigre, his nickname for me, it means Tiger in Spanish. "How was your first day of school?" I walk over to him to see that he is standing on a stool, hanging up a painting of a fruit bowl on the wall.

"It was pretty good." he looks down at me, disbelief in his eyes.

"Really?" he has always known that I get picked on in school. He has gotten many calls from the school about me getting bullied by the other kids. It's kind of understandable for him not to believe me when I say that school was alright.

"Yeah, I don't have many classes with the kids who made fun of me and the people I do share my classes with seem pretty cool."

"I see, anybody in particular that you think is cool?" I smile when I think of the obvious person to answer his question.

"Well there is this one person, she is really-"

"Wait, she?" my uncle looks at me, mischief and joy lighting up his face as his smile becomes so large that his eyes are almost practically shut.

"Don't look at me like that, okay? She's just a friend." He chuckles at me.

"Okay, what is this 'friend's' name?"

"Her name is Colomba, and she is really cool." he chuckles at me again.

"That's good to hear." he steps down from the stool, his smile still on his face. "I have something for you to celebrate your first day back in school." he walks to the other side of the store and steps behind the counter, pulling out a small box from a drawer. He holds it out to me and I take it with eager hands.

"Thanks Uncle, what is it?"

"Open it and find out." I lift the lid off of the

tiny box to see what looks like an old-fashioned war medal sitting in the box. A large, silver coin is held to the pin by a black and blue striped ribbon. When I take it out of the box and take a closer look at it, I can see what is on the medal. A crow is carved into the silver medal, its wings are spread out as it is perched on a branch, its mouth open wide as if it is letting out a cry.

"This is really cool, what is it? Where did you get it?"

"An older woman came in, wanting to sell it to me. He couldn't tell me anything about it, except that he found it years ago. I gave him a few dollars for it and he went on his way. I've been trying to find out more about it since this morning, but I can't find anything. Since I can't really sell it without having any information about it, or even tell my customers what it is, I thought you might want it instead." I smile at him, I have always liked antiques, something I got from my uncle. I've been collecting antiques for a few years now, mainly small things like pocket watches, little gadgets, and old war medals. Something like this could easily fit into my collection.

"Thank you so much." I wrap my arms around him in a tight hug.

"No problem, Tigre. I knew you would love it." The bell above the front door rings, I let go of my uncle as he goes off to help the customer that just walked in the door.

I go into the back of the store and up a flight of stairs to enter the apartment that my uncle and I share. Passing through the living room, I head straight into my room and sit down on my bed, looking at the medal my uncle gave me. It looks extremely old, maybe even more than a hundred years old. The metal is dirty, and a bit worn down, the detailing on it has faded significantly, it's as if it hasn't been cleaned in decades. The fabric that is attached to the medal is frayed and the color has faded, like it has gone into the washer a few times too many.

It will take some serious work to make this thing look better, but I think it will be worth it in the end. Uncle Diego may not know much about what it is or where it came from, but I think that this might be something special.

As I stare at it, something strange happens, the dirt on the medal starts falling off and lands on my sheets in a fine powder. My eyes open wide when all the dirt has disappeared, and the medal looks as if it is brand new. The color has returned to the fabric and the detailing on the medal looks perfect. I squint my eyes to try and figure out what happened, but then the medal begins to glow. When the medal becomes so bright that I have to close my eyes, I drop it on the bed, covering my eyes with my hands. When the light is no longer shining, I open my eyes to see that the medal is still sitting on my bed as if nothing has happened.

Looking around my room, nothing seems unusual, that is, until I look at my dresser. Perched on top of a lamp on my dresser is a large crow, I jump back in shock when I see it. The bird is staring at me, it doesn't seem afraid of me at all like most birds would in this situation. How did this bird get in my room? None of my windows are open so how did it get in? I move to the other side of my room to open my window to try and get it back outside when the bird opens its beak and speaks to me.

"Good evening Master, my name is Shadow, I am your guide." The crow has a woman's voice, a soft, gentle voice, a voice full of wisdom. I stare at the crow with my mouth wide open, my heart racing in my chest.

Did I actually hear that coming from the bird or is someone trying to play a cruel joke on me? I wouldn't put it past Alex to try and pull a prank on me, to make me think that I am going crazy, but I don't think that he could pull off something this clever. Oh my gosh, it feels like I'm going to throw up.

"As long as you wear that medal, I will always be there to help you." The crow flies off my lamp and lands on my shoulder. I freeze when I feel the bird on my shoulder. I want to swat it away in my fear but all I can think is that I can feel it, the bird is real, I'm not dreaming this! The bird continues to explain, "This medal gives you special powers;" as the bird talks, I watch it move its mouth, trying to see if there is some kind of microphone attached to it somehow, but there isn't one. I can hear the words coming from the bird's mouth. This is actually happening.

"You can use it to summon me so that I can do what you want in the form of a shadow or I can help you take control of other people and give them abilities beyond that of a normal person." my eyes open wide in surprise and I feel myself smile despite the strange circumstances. This bird gives away super powers?

"So, you can give people superpowers?" the bird nods its head at me. "Well why can't you give me superpowers?" The bird lowers its head.

"I'm afraid it doesn't work that way, you can only give the powers to other people." Okay, if this talking crow is real, maybe what it's saying is true too, maybe I should follow what it says. Who knows what this crow, Shadow, can do for me.

"But I can make them do whatever I want?"

"Yes, but you must be responsible with this ability. Having a power like this can easily make you forget what is right and wrong, just remember that these powers should be used for the betterment of the world and not just yourself. The only reason that I have appeared to you in the first place instead of your uncle, or the man who sold it to your uncle, is because I could feel that you were the one destined to wear the Crow Medal. You have a good heart that wants to do good in the world, to make this world a better place." I can hear what the bird is saying, but I'm not really paying attention.

I can finally get what I want with these powers, I can make all of those people at school leave me alone, or even better, I can actually have friends. I can't even remember the last time I had someone who I could call a real friend. Colomba might be a friend to me right now, but she might stop being nice to me when she sees how everyone else treats me. I've had that happen before.

When I was in Kindergarten, before they all started teasing me, I did have a friend, Alex. Despite what he is now, back then he was my best friend, my only friend. We used to play together every day on the playground, we would eat lunch together, and when we had to have partners to do anything in class or gym we would always choose each other, but then something changed.

One day in class the teacher praised me for being the only one to pass a math test that everyone else got a C or below on. When the teacher was done speaking, someone from the back of the room yelled out, calling me a nerd. Everyone joined him in laughing at me, even Alex. He didn't even seem conflicted about laughing at his friend. Before the teacher could stop everyone from laughing I clearly heard him call me a teacher's pet. The entire class got in trouble that day, everyone had to stay after school for an hour to do math worksheets except for me. The teacher probably thought that she was doing the right thing by punishing them, but that only made them hate me.

After that Alex and I no longer played on the playground, he would stay as far away from me as possible unless he was teasing me or playing some kind of prank on me. We no longer had lunch together, I ate all by myself. And whenever we needed a partner for class or gym, I was the odd man out while everyone else had a partner.

Slowly Alex became the worst bully of all, I doubt he even remembers how we used to be best friends. I bet he doesn't even care to remember anything that would make him seem less cool. After that day in Kindergarten I stopped having friends; every once in a while, someone new would move into town and would start talking to me, but that never lasted long. They would see how other people treated me and they would leave me so that they wouldn't have to face the same outcast treatment that I have had to deal with all of these years.

I close my eyes, trying to get rid of that sad memory. I want to forget it, but I know I can't. You can't just wish away a sad memory. Colomba flashes through my mind and I smile despite the pain in my heart. I know that I have only known her for a day, but she is the kindest person I have ever met. I don't want to lose her like I have lost every other "friend" that I have ever made. I don't want to lose what little I have left. Looking at the crow called Shadow, I smile at her.

"Alright, my friend, tell me all about this medal."

Chapter Nine
Colomba-
Superpowers Are Hard

The first week of school went pretty well. I love all of my classes, I like most of the people I have my classes with, and I've been learning a lot of interesting things so far. I think I will really enjoy myself this year. I had planned on spending my first weekend out of school hanging out with my new friends since they were all going to go to the park to hang out and possibly see a movie later on together, but Nonna has different plans for me today.

Right now, Nonna is training me on how to use my new superpowers in our backyard. Since we live in the country, and Dad is working today, we are all alone, and nobody can see us. Nobody will see me in my Silver Dove form and find out my true identity. Even if someone were to drive down the road in front of my house, they still wouldn't be able to see me. There are huge trees blocking anybody's view into the backyard. I am completely safe to be myself here.

Nonna is teaching me how to fly right now, and boy is it hard. The highest I've been able to fly so far is eight feet off the ground, and then I crashed only a few seconds after getting that high. I just can't seem to get the hang of flapping my wings. It feels weird enough having wings coming out of my back, it feels even weirder to try and use them.

"Beat your wings faster or else you won't have enough energy to pick yourself off the ground." Nonna says as I try to follow her instructions.

As I beat my wings, it creates a strong gust of wind around me that sends leaves on the ground flying away. "That's it Tesoro, just a little bit more, and keep your arms closer to your sides so that they won't get in the way of your wings." My wings flap hard and fast, it almost feels like I am trying to create a tornado with my wings with the current of wind I'm creating. Debris is now flying away furiously from the power of my wings. When I feel as if I can't beat my wings any faster, my feet are no longer touching the ground.

Looking down, I laugh out loud in joy when I see that I am five feet off the ground, my joy is short lived though since I immediately fall to the ground for the billionth time. Nonna calls over to me from the lawn chair she's sitting on.

"I think that's enough practice for right now, how about you come over here for a minute and have some lemonade with me?" I smile, grateful that she's giving me a break. Picking myself off the ground, I walk over to her and take the glass of lemonade that she holds out to me as I take a seat in a lawn chair beside her. I sigh, glad to finally relax after working so hard.

"Can you please explain everything about this

pin again, and the powers it gives me?" Nonna smiles, she has already explained it to me a bunch of times, but she knows that this is all still pretty weird for me.

"The pin transforms you into Silver Dove when you place your hand over it and say the magic words. When you are Silver Dove, you have super strength, you can easily pick up a car if you want to. You have to be careful about that, though, since having super strength can be hard to control. You are also indestructible. With your wings, obviously, you can fly, but you can fly at a very impressive speed, around a hundred miles per hour. When you transform, a sword appears with your armor. You can fight with this, and if you lose it in the fight, it will come back to you if you concentrate on bringing it back. Those are your powers as Silver Dove, remember to use them wisely." she smiles softly at me and I know that she's hoping that I won't ask her the same question again.

"Do I have any kind of weaknesses as Silver Dove?" she nods at me.

"Yes, only one though, if you get too tired while in the form of Silver Dove, you will transform back into your normal self. This can be a major problem since your identity is supposed to remain a secret, and if this happens while you are flying you can get seriously hurt if you are flying too high. Make sure that you end the fight quickly so that you won't get too exhausted. Oh," her eyes open wide as if she has suddenly remembered something, "I forgot to mention this: after the fight is over, there will usually be some damage from the fight, so you have the special ability to fix whatever damage you, or the person you have been fighting, caused. I can show you how to do this later, but we need to focus on the basics first, like the flying lessons we're doing now." I nod my head, trying to wrap my mind around all of this.

"Okay, I just have a few more questions." Nonna chuckles at me, knowing that I have more than just "a few more questions" to ask her. "Why didn't you give this pin to Mom, why did you wait before you gave it to me?" Her happy expression fades, and deep sadness enters her eyes.

"Your mother was never a very healthy girl." I look away from Nonna, feeling guilty for asking her about Mom. She is always sad when I bring her up. My mom died from cancer when I was a baby, and it still hurts my dad and Nonna to think about her even though it was many years ago. Thinking about her still hurts me too, even though I was too young to even remember my mom.

"I could never give her the pin because she was never healthy. I was too focused on keeping her strong enough to go outside and play as a child to even think about making her a superhero. She was always fighting off her cancer, even as a child, it would come back no matter how hard we tried to fight it. I couldn't let her fight villains as well as her cancer." I quickly change the subject, hoping to lighten up the dark atmosphere around us.

"What about Dad, why can't we tell him about the pin?" Nonna looks down at the lemonade that she is holding with both hands. She appears uncomfortable by what she feels like she needs to say.

"Your father wouldn't really agree with what I am training you to be. He wouldn't want you to go out and fight evil. He is very protective of you, he feels that you are all that he has left of your mother." Nonna looks off into the distance, looking out at the farmland beyond our backyard. "You were too young to remember this, but when you first started wanting to take martial arts when you were younger your father was very against it, he thought that you would get hurt. It took a long time, but I convinced him that it would be good for you and help you make friends, as well as defend yourself later on." She shakes her head slowly, thinking about that memory.

"If we told him about the pin, then he would never let you transform into Silver Dove again. He would be trying to protect you, but he would be taking away a part of your destiny. I know that you are meant to be the next Silver Dove, I can feel it in my old bones." I smile as I gently hug her, something pretty hard to do since I'm still having a hard time controlling my wings and they tend to get in the way whenever I try to hug her.

She is right, Dad has always been very protective of me. He always seems to prefer that I stay at home instead of going out. It will be difficult keeping this secret from him, not just because it is a huge secret, but also because I tell my dad everything. There have never been any secrets between us. Keeping this from him will be one of the hardest things I have ever done. After a moment of silence, I ask her a question that has been bothering me ever since she gave me the pin.

"Why did you give this pin to me now? I'm still pretty young to be a superhero, why now?"

"It's going to sound stupid," she grins at me, blushing slightly, "but I feel as if something is about to happen, something bad that will need Silver Dove's help to solve. I don't know what it is, but I thought it would be best to give it to you now so that we would be prepared for when it happens." I still don't feel as if she has answered my question.

"I don't understand, what could possibly happen that everyone would need me? Couldn't the police or someone else help if something bad happens?" She nods at my words, knowing that it makes sense to ask this.

"Yes, the police can be helpful in most bad situations, but when it comes to something magical, like your pin, they can't really solve it, they are powerless. That will be the time that they need us." I feel my heart race.

"You mean that there's more magic in the world than just in my pin?" She chuckles at my surprise.

"Yes, Tesoro, there is, only a little bit though. The last bit of magic left in the world is kept in a few magical objects, one of which is your pin. I have seen only three of these objects in my life, and I think that those are the only magical items left in the world." I feel my heart leap in excitement.

"Well, where did those objects come from?" she sighs softly and looks up, trying to figure out a way to explain this.

"Centuries ago, there was still magic in the world, but only a few people were able to control it.

Most used their magic for good, others for evil. Those who were good had the responsibility of stopping those who tried to use their powers for evil, that was how it was for many years. One day, there was only one keeper of magic left and she knew that she couldn't hold onto her magic forever, so she placed her magic into three magical pins that could only be worn by those who were worthy of the power by having a good heart." She smiles at me warmly.

"I am so proud to know that the pin feels that you are worthy of this power. I believe that is enough questions for now, I don't want to overload you with information. Since you've had a few minutes to rest, let's try flying again." I let out a faint sigh, not eager to fall on my face again in a failed attempt at flight. I want to hear more about my pin and these other magical objects, but I have a feeling that Nonna wouldn't tell me about them even if I asked, so I remain silent.

Even though I don't want to do this, I get up from the lawn chair and go back to the field in front of the chairs. Opening my wings out wide, I prepare to try and fly again. I look at my wings, still surprised to see them coming out of my back. When I stare at them, it feels like I am in a strange, but wonderful, dream that I will soon wake up from. I take a deep breath, trying to focus so that I can fly again.

"Remember, when you fly, you need to let go of all your fear. Don't be afraid of falling, don't be afraid of anything. You are in control, there is no reason to be afraid." Taking in a deep breath, I follow her advice. I get rid of any thoughts of falling, I only think about opening my wings and flapping them like a bird. I feel the muscles in my wings moving, and after a few moments, I feel my feet leave the ground.

Opening my eyes, I look down to see that I am now over ten feet above the ground, my Nonna is smiling up at me, and I laugh out loud in joy. I can't believe it, I'm actually flying!

I shout out in my excitement and start flying fast in loops and diving down to the ground only to open my wings up again right before I hit the ground, sending me back up into the sky. This is incredible! I close my eyes, enjoying the feeling of the wind rushing against my face. I hear my Nonna trying to yell something to me, but I can't understand what it is since I'm up too high now. Opening my eyes, I look down at her and yell, "What did you say, Nonna?"

I'm not quite sure what she says, but it almost sounds like "look out." Looking ahead of me I suddenly realize that "look out" was exactly what she was trying to say to me. I quickly cover my head with my arms as I crash into the branches of a huge oak tree. The branches snap against my body as I go through them, but they slow me down until I am at a complete stop, stuck in the tree, my wings caught in the web of branches. I am suddenly extremely grateful that one of my superpowers is invincibility, or else I would have been seriously hurt from that crash. Through the branches beneath me, I can see my Nonna rushing over and peering through the leaves, trying to find me.

"Colomba, are you in there?" I feel my cheeks growing warm, and I know that I'm blushing in my embarrassment.

"Yeah, I'm here."

"Are you alright, is anything hurt?"

"Just my pride." she smiles up at me, chuckling.

"That's alright, your pride will heal. Come on down Tesoro, and we'll try this again. Maybe this time we can try it with our eyes open." I can't help myself, I laugh at her joke as I slip through the branches to land on the ground beside her. We walk back to our backyard so that I can try again, hopefully this time I won't do anything stupid.

<u>Chapter Ten</u>
Luis-
The Power of the
Medal

The first week of school has actually been pretty great. I get to see Colomba every day since we share a few classes. I haven't really had any run-ins with Alex or that one girl who screamed at me the first day, and I think that Colomba might even see me as a friend. On the first day of school, I walked into the lunchroom, not sure where I could sit that would be safe. I wasn't sure where I could sit down where someone from my old school wouldn't tease me.

In middle school I would eat my lunch alone behind the school under an old oak tree to make sure that nobody could find me. Nobody ever sat with me back there, I would spend my time reading a book or watching the birds and squirrels live their lives in the field behind the school. It was a lonely place, but it was a safe place, and at the time that's all I wanted.

I didn't have to worry though about finding a

safe place to eat my lunch. I had only walked a few feet into the cafeteria when I heard a sweet voice call out my name. I turned around to see Colomba sitting down at a table and gesturing for me to sit with her and her friends. I sat with her that lunch period and had the time of my life, not only because her friends are really nice and Colomba let me have some of her lunch, which she had made herself (and it tasted fantastic), but because I got to sit next to her. I was quiet for most of the time since practically everyone at that table was a stranger to me, but Colomba always made sure that I was involved in the conversation, asking my opinion and helping me loosen up. She is amazing, I will never meet anyone as kind as her.

Right now, Shadow is flying above me as I stand in the parking lot behind my uncle's antique shop. It is almost dark outside, so I can't see anyone nearby. She is circling in the air, making sure that there is nobody around to see me before she starts teaching me how to use my new powers. Slowly, she flies lower and lower until she lands on my shoulder.

"Alright Master, there is nobody close to us, we are safe to train in peace." I smile at Shadow, still unsure about how I feel about all of this.

"Okay, where do we start?"

"First, I will need to explain a few things. If you ever need to summon me, all you have to do is place your hand over the medal, and I will come to help you. Just make sure that you are alone when you speak to me since others can see me as well, nobody but those who hold a magical object can hear my voice. If you speak to me in the presence of others, then they will believe that you are crazy since you are talking to a bird. Many years ago, one of the previous owners of the medal was burned at the stake because a few people heard him speak to me and they thought that he was a witch." I involuntarily flinch at the thought of that happening to someone, what a horrible way to die. Shadow continues on with her explanation as if what she just said wasn't very horrific.

"When I am with you, I can give you special abilities and transform you into the superhero the Crow, but once you transform, I will no longer be there, and you will be on your own. Once in the form of the Crow, you can control shadow creatures that you create. They will do whatever you say without question. To create these shadow creatures, you must focus on what they look like, and don't just give a vague idea of their appearance. Be as detailed as possible, so detailed that they live in your mind. Only once they are real in your mind will they come to life in the real world. These creatures can only disappear by you willing them to disappear or by an incredible force destroying them." Wow, I can only imagine what I will do once I can create these shadow creatures. I can probably make Alex wet himself in terror with one of those the next time he tries to mess with anyone.

"You can also give special abilities to other people and you can have them use their abilities to do whatever you ask of them. In the form of the Crow, you can fly with a set of dark wings, and you will appear with a staff in your hand. This staff is unbreakable, you can use it to defeat your enemies. I warn you though, your only weakness is that you can't get too tired or else your powers will fade, and you will transform back into your normal form. Be very cautious and listen to your body, if you start feeling tired, do not exert yourself, just let yourself relax." I nod at her, still feeling very confused.

"You said that when I transform into the Crow, you disappear, where do you go?"

"To let you transform, I become a part of you, giving you all of my magic so that you can use your abilities for the betterment of the world." A sudden idea comes to me, if these powers were given to me to help the world, I must have been given these powers for a reason. Destiny must be on my side, and I think I know how I want to help the world.

"Shadow?" I practically whisper this, suddenly uncomfortable by what is going on in my mind. I feel embarrassed by what I am going to ask Shadow, since it will probably sound ridiculous to her, but I feel like I need to ask her this.

"Yes, Master?" Shadow tips her head to the side, confused by my sudden shyness.

"These powers were given to me to help the world. Can I use them to help stop the bullying in my school? I've always been picked on at school, and I don't want anyone to have to go through that like I did. I know that this sounds stupid, but I want to help the people like me, the ones too afraid to stand up for themselves." I'm pretty sure that birds can't smile, but it feels like Shadow is smiling warmly at me.

"Of course, you can use your powers to help

them, that is a very good use for your powers. Just remember that you need to use your powers wisely. Even if you are trying to do the right thing, you can mess it up if you don't do it the right way. With something like trying to stop bullying, it can be very difficult figuring out how to make it stop." I nod to her, only partially understanding what she means.

"Alright, Shadow, let's practice, transform me into the Crow. I want to see what I can do." Shadow nods her head at me before she takes off from my shoulder and starts flying around me, flying faster and faster until she is nothing more than a dark blur. I blink my eyes for the slightest second and she is gone, looking around myself, she is nowhere in sight. My mind rushes as I try to figure out where she could have gone and then I understand. She told me that she disappears whenever she transforms into the Crow, she becomes a part of me.

I lift my hand to see that I am wearing black gloves that I didn't have on a second ago, in one of my gloved hands is a long staff made from dark wood. Staring down at myself I can see that I am wearing black clothes. Frantically looking around I notice a parked car nearby. Running over to it, I glance into the side mirror and gasp in surprise at what I see. The person in the mirror has on a black mask that has what looks like a bird's beak on it. The mask appears to be made of some kind of black metal, while the rest of my costume is made of leather. My appearance surprises me, but what really catches my eye is that I now have wings coming out of my back. The wings are black, just like the rest of my costume, and are covered in feathers like a bird. Chuckling softly in surprise, I reach my hand back and stroke the feathers, it tickles me a bit to do so, my wings are as soft as a cloud.

"Wow Shadow this is amazing I-!" I turn around, forgetting that she is no longer with me. Remembering what she said before, I know that she won't be coming back until I transform back into my usual self.

Holding the staff out in front of me, I feel the weight of it in my hand. In a quick, sudden movement, I swing the staff out and smash a bottle that had been sitting on top of a trashcan. I laugh out loud as the broken glass spreads out on the concrete at my feet. In my joy I close my eyes as I concentrate on my wings, trying to flap them. Using all of my concentration, I feel my wings beating in a regular, but slow, rhythm. I focus harder and the wings start moving faster and faster. My heart skips a beat when I feel my feet leave the pavement. Opening my eyes I look down to see that I am several feet off the ground. Laughing as the adrenaline pumps through my body, I soar high into the darkening sky, completely thrilled by the rush of the wind against my face. I feel as if I could touch the stars that are just beginning to appear above me. I want to do it, but I know I can't. Slowly, I bring myself lower until I am only a few feet off the ground.

Glancing to my side, I notice a plank of wood from a carpentry project that my uncle had used, but apparently no longer needs since it is propped up against our trashcan. A sudden thought hits me, looking down at my hand, I ball my gloved hand into a fist and strike out against the plank of wood and my hand is engulfed in a sudden wave of pain. Waving my hand in the air frantically, I let out a few yelps of agony.

Okay, so I don't have super strength and I can still feel pain, so I am not impervious. That kinda stinks, but my other powers are pretty awesome, so I guess I can live with it. Shaking my hurt hand, I take a deep breath, trying to alleviate the pain. When the pain is bearable, I remember something that Shadow told me, I can create shadow creatures who will do whatever I say.

Closing my eyes again, I do what Shadow told me to do, I focus on what these creatures will look like, I try to imagine every detail about them. Thinking hard, I picture these creatures to be a few inches taller than me and be incredibly strong, they won't have a lot of detail to them since I don't want to have to focus so hard on them in case I have to make a lot of them. They will look like giant dogs. Dogs have always scared me, so I want everyone who faces my shadow creatures to be just as scared of them as me. They will be solid black, like the shadows they are made of, and have burning red eyes. Sharp teeth will poke out of their snarling lips and they will have a booming bark that will send shivers down anyone's spine.

With that picture in mind, I open my eyes to see what looks like a blob made of shadows standing in front of me. I step back in surprise when I first see it, but then disappointment overwhelms me as the blob just stands there, not doing anything. I guess I didn't focus on it hard enough. The shadow blob seems to blow away in the wind as I will it away. Closing my eyes again, I focus as hard as I can on the image that I came up with. I will keep working on this tonight until I get it right, even if I have to stay up all night I will do it. My teeth grind in concentration as I make one shadow blob after another, they disappear almost as quickly as they come, but I won't stop. I won't stop until I have perfection.

<u>Chapter Eleven</u>
Colomba- My Life at School

Everything always seems so perfect when I walk into the front doors of my school. I love coming here every day. I get to see all of my wonderful friends and I have interesting classes to go to. Also, this school has a great library that I can go to every day, which is pretty important to someone who loves to read as much as I do. Every day just seems to get better and better, maybe Nonna was wrong. Maybe there isn't anything bad coming. How could anything bad happen when everything is going so well? Everyone is always so pleasant to me. It's hard to imagine that any of them would do anything evil to someone else so that Silver Dove would have to intervene. I just don't understand what could give Nonna this feeling that something bad is about to happen.

Even though this is only the second week of the school year, I already know where everything is. I haven't gotten lost since my first day of school.

I am sitting in class now, reading a book since I am finished with the assignment that everyone else is still working on. All around me, people are scribbling their answers on paper or staring down at the worksheet with thoughtful expressions. It is peaceful in the room, but that doesn't last. The silence of the room is broken as the ground begins to rumble beneath my feet. I grab the desk frantically, terrified as the books start falling off the shelves and the other students begin to scream, some try to run out the door, but for some reason it won't open.

My ears ring and ache when a massive cracking sound seems to explode within the room. I glance up to look where the sound had come from to see what looks like massive claws coming in through the ceiling. I try to open my mouth to scream, but nothing comes out, I am too terrified to make a sound. Chunks of plaster and ceiling tiles rain down on all of the students, we rush under our desks as the ceiling gets torn up by the claws. I swallow my fear and look up from beneath the desk to see a massive monster holding the remains of what had been the ceiling.

The monster looks like a massive black lizard the size of a mountain, its scales are the color of the night sky while its teeth that poke out from beneath its lips are white but tinged red with blood. The creature tosses away the remains of the ceiling and throws its head back in a roar that makes everyone cover their ears. Even though I cover my ears, they still hurt from the power of that ferocious roar.

When it finishes that terrible sound, it looks

down at all of us, saliva dripping from its fangs in hunger. Everyone tries to run and find a place to hide as the monster lowers one of its humongous arms, its claws stretched out to grab something. As the creature reaches closer to me, I try to squirm out from under my desk, but my shirt catches on a bolt on the leg of my desk. Pulling forcefully at my shirt doesn't help, before I know it, the creature has me in its scaly hand and lifts me up toward its face.

Struggling frantically in the monster's grip doesn't do me any good. I slam my fist against its fingers, kick wherever I can reach, and I even try to bite its hand, but the monster still doesn't release me. My heart is pounding frantically as tears run down my face. I beg the monster to let me go, but it only brings me right up to its face so that I can look it right in the eyes.

The eyes are golden, but it isn't a bright, cheerful gold, more of a dull, lifeless gold mixed with a murky brown. I fall silent when I look in its eyes, knowing that it is useless to try and beg anymore. When I look in its eyes, I know that I am going to die.

The monster opens its mouth, bringing me closer and closer to the fangs as my sobbing grows louder. I open my mouth to release one last scream of horror when a loud bang makes me jump.

Opening my eyes, I glance around myself to see that I am still in the classroom. Looking up, the ceiling is still above me and there is no monster in sight. In front of me, one of the other students is picking up a book that they had apparently dropped, that must have been what had made the banging sound.

I rub my eyes frantically, a little frustrated with myself. It was just a dream stupid. If you know it is a dream, then why is your heart still racing like horse? I ask myself this, but I feel as if I already know the answer. It is because of what my Nonna said, something bad is coming and I have to stop it. I want to groan in misery, but I need to stay quiet or else the teacher will get mad at me. How can I stop something bad if I am so terrified by a bad dream? I am such a baby.

My Nonna should have picked someone else to give these powers to, I am not brave enough to do something like this. I won't know what to do when something does happen, I will get scared and hide. I do not deserve to have these powers. If I know my Nonna though, she won't let me give it back to her, she would convince me to keep it and try my best. Even though I want to give it back, I know I can't because I know that it would disappoint her if I did and I would rather do anything than disappoint Nonna.

Taking in a deep breath, I know that I have to do something to get rid of my fear. To do that, I need to know what I am up against. I need to know what this horrible thing is that Nonna is talking about so that I can figure out how to stop it. Thinking carefully, I try to think of anything bad happening at this school, but nothing comes to mind. To me, everything seems perfect at school, I love coming here every day.

I know that if I need to figure this out, then I need to ask someone else if they have noticed anything unusual. I am not a very observant person, I probably wouldn't notice a bird flying in front of my face unless someone pointed it out to me. I am always so focused on what I am doing that everything else just disappears, it's something I need to work on. I need to ask someone far more observant than me.

Picking up my book again, I try to read as the last ten minutes of class passes, but when I am done reading a page, I realize that I haven't paid attention to a single word. My mind is still trapped in my dream and I can't think of anything else. Giving up on my book, I set it down and rest my head against my desk, trying to clear the dark memory of that dream from my thoughts.

Chapter Twelve
Luis-
My Pain at
School

I hate walking through the doors of this school. There are so many people that pick on me. Alex finds every chance to bully me, and none of the teachers do anything about it. Just yesterday I was walking down the hallway and Alex came around a corner and slapped me on the back of the head as he passed. A teacher was only a few feet away from us, and I'm pretty sure he saw the whole thing, yet he did nothing. He just looked away from us and went into his classroom as if nothing happened. The only thing that makes it all worthwhile is Colomba. She tries to make every day fun for everyone she talks to. She's a bright ray of sunshine in this dark school.

As I walk down the hallway, heading to my next class, someone sticks out their foot, and I trip over it. My books fly out of my hand as I fall to the ground. Several people laugh as I pick my stuff back up. Nobody helps me gather my stuff, they just continue walking around me, heading to their next classes. Once I have my stuff together, I continue walking to class as if nothing happened.

Passing by the girl's bathroom, I see a girl that I recognize from middle school slipping inside, tears beginning to stream down her face. Before she makes it into the room I hear her mutter under her breath, "How could they say that about me on A-Streamer?"

A-Streamer is a social media website that's pretty popular around here, practically everyone in school has an account on it. I used to have one before Alex and my other bullies made it unbearable for me, so I deleted it after only having it for a week. Not too long ago I made an account with a fake name, I don't really use it that much, I just keep it to stay up to date on things that are going on around town. Opening it up on my phone, I look up the name of the girl I had seen go into the bathroom and I easily find her page. It doesn't take me long to find out why she was so upset, written all over her page are horrible things; people calling her fat, a freak, and a loser among a lot of other stuff that I know from personal experience hurts whenever you hear someone say it to you.

Shaking my head, I stuff my phone back into my back pocket. This is why I want to use my powers to help bullied kids; so that I will never have to see someone in tears because of what somebody said. So that people won't be forced to sit by themselves at lunch because nobody wants to associate with a freak. Nobody should ever feel that they are worthless in the eyes of their peers.

When I turn around a corner, I see someone and

instantly everything feels better again.

"Hey Colomba." I call out to her, she turns to look at me and gives me her perfect smile.

"Hi Luis, how are you?" I almost told her that I wasn't doing so well considering what just happened, but she looks so happy right now that I don't want to ruin her day with my problems.

"I'm doing fine I suppose, how are you Colomba?"

"I'm fantastic, I love this school, everyone is so friendly."

I'm surprised by her words, has she not seen what I've seen? Kids are getting picked on all the time at this school, but I guess none of this happens to her. Nobody would want to tease someone as kind as her.

"Really?" I ask her without thinking. She looks up at me, pain in her gaze.

"What do you mean, don't you like it here too? Is there something I can do to help?" It warms my heart to hear her say that she wants to help me, but I don't want her to know about what I go through every day. I don't want her to think I'm some weak, pathetic loser like everyone else in this school. Instead of telling her the truth, I give her a white lie.

"Uh... no I'm happy too, I'm glad that you're happy." her smile returns after a moment as she thankfully changes the subject to an assignment that we had for our English class. I go with the conversation, but I make a mistake when I explain one reason I would like to live in my books.

"Yeah, I would love to have things end out perfectly like it does in stories, riding off in the sunset and getting the girl in the end."

"I'm sorry Luis, what was that last thing you said?" Oh, I didn't mean to say that last part out loud. I'm such an idiot.

"Nothing, I didn't say anything, we should hurry to class, we don't want to be late." We're already several minutes early, but that was the first thing I could think of to change the subject. I open the door to the classroom for her and we both sit down beside each other in the front row. When we sit down, she shocks me by asking something that I would never have expected.

"Hey, Luis, do you know about anything... bad that has been going on lately?"

Not wanting to look like a wimp by talking about how I am getting bullied, I lie, "No, I don't think so, why do you ask?"

I feel bad about lying to her, but I don't want her to worry about me.

"Sorry Luis, it's just that I have a funny feeling that something bad is about to happen, do you know what I mean?" I nod my head at her.

"Yeah, I think I know what you mean, I get those kinds of feelings a lot." She looks at me, a bit surprised.

"Really, you do?"

"Yeah, I always get them before something bad is about to happen, it's kind of helpful. It's like my mind is warning me. Maybe I'm a Jedi, and the Force is warning me of imminent danger, maybe someone is about to strike the Millennium Falcon or something." I'm surprised she actually laughs at such a nerdy Star Wars joke.

The teacher ruins our time together by walking through the door and starting class. As she starts taking up everyone's reports I look over at Colomba, wondering what bad things could happen to her that would give her these strange feelings.

Eventually class ends, and Colomba and I go our separate ways to head to our next classes. The rest of the day was uneventful. I finished my classes and then rode the bus back home. I walk into my uncle's store and then head upstairs to our apartment. Only when I am in the safety of my room do I place my hand over my Crow Medal and Shadow appears on my dresser. I know that she's a bird, and birds don't really have facial expressions, but she somehow seems happy to see me.

"Hello, Master, did you have a good day at school?" I smile at her as I unpack my backpack to get out my homework. "Yeah, today was pretty alright, a few kids messed with me, but I got to hang out with Colomba today, so that made everything better." Shadow nods her head at me.

"Yes, I saw everything that happened today. It pained me to see everything that the other students did to you, but I am happy that this girl, Colomba, makes you happy." I smile, feeling my face grow warm and I know I'm blushing.

"Yeah, Colomba is pretty awesome."

Shadow flies off my dresser to land on my shoulder. "Master, when we first met you said that you intended to use your new abilities with the Medal to help other people in your position, people who are being bullied. When and how do you plan on doing this?" I don't look at Shadow as I start organizing the homework papers in my hands. I don't know how to answer her question, so I answer her honestly.

"I'm not sure, I don't really know how I'm going to do this, I've never had superpowers before you know?" Shadow chuckles softly at my sarcasm. "I suppose when the time comes, I will know how I will take care of the problem. I want to help people with these powers, and I want to do it right. I don't want to make a mistake with this."

"It is impossible not to make a mistake," Shadow says in her motherly voice. "Everyone makes mistakes. That is part of being human. It is alright to make mistakes, but it reveals a truly amazing human being who can admit their mistakes and try to fix them." I nod at Shadow, not really sure how to respond to something as wise as that.

A smile starts to form on my lips when I think of something. "Hey Shadow?"

"Yes, Master?"

I feel awkward about asking this, but I really want to know her answer. "Do you think that, when I use these powers to help people, Colomba might start to like me?"

Shadow cocks her head to the side in her confusion. "I do not understand, Colomba already likes you very much."

"No, not like as a friend, but I mean like as a... a boyfriend. Do you think that she might like me like that if I use my powers to help people like in a comic book or a movie? Do you think that if I use my powers to help people that she might respect and admire me enough to end up loving me?" For an entire minute Shadow remains silent, lost in thought. I think I see pity flash in her eyes for the slightest second before she conceals it. Eventually, she flies off my shoulder to land on my bed.

"I don't know, people should admire those who do good deeds, but I do not know if she will fall in love with you because of it."

"But do you think there's a chance that she might love me, maybe not today, but someday?" Shadow looks at me with sad eyes, the eyes of someone trying not to disappoint someone they care about.

"Perhaps one day. When I look at Colomba, I see a girl who has a very strong idea of what she wants. She is an ambitious girl, but I don't think that romance is one of her ambitions." Shadow states this in a matter-of-fact tone that makes me a little angry.

"So, you're saying that I don't have a chance with her?"

"No, I didn't mean that at all." Shadow shakes her head at me. "I'm merely saying that she doesn't love you now, but that may change one day. Just be patient. Sometimes fate can be in your favor, but if she doesn't fall for you, then I know that you will love another. You are a good person and deserve to have someone who loves you just as much as you love them. I have not been with you for very long, but I can see that you have a great capacity for love." I lower my head, feeling ashamed of myself.

"I'm sorry Shadow, I didn't mean to snap at you. It's just hard, you know?" Shadow nods her head again.

"I believe I understand, Master. You care for her, but you are afraid to tell her your true feelings since that might affect the relationship you have now, which you wouldn't want to lose for anything in the world. You want her to be happy, even though you know that she may not care for you in the same way. You will do anything for her, even though you probably won't get anything out of it. Am I right?"

I clear my throat, and I know that I'm blushing again. "Yeah that sounds about right to me."

Shadow flies onto my shoulder again as I walk across my room with my homework to sit at my desk. "Don't be embarrassed by this. You should never feel ashamed by how you feel. Besides, 'it is better to have loved and lost than to never have loved at all.' That's how that old saying goes. It is a very old saying, but a very true one." I smile at Shadow, trying to feel comforted by her words, but I don't.

It is nice of her to say all of that, but I want Colomba to love me just as much as I love her, and I don't want her to see me the same way everyone else does, the pathetic, nerdy loser that deserves to get picked on. I need to use my powers to end the bullying at this school as soon as possible, for one reason, to end the suffering of all the other students like me who get picked on every day, and the other reason is that I don't want Colomba to see me getting bullied. I can't let her see the way everyone bullies me, I can't let her see me as someone weak like everyone else does. I want her to see me as someone she wants to be around, someone she can care about. I want to end the bullying at my school.

That is what I want more than anything, but I also want it to end so that Colomba won't pity me; is that so wrong?

As I start working on my homework, I have a hard time concentrating on it because my mind keeps drifting to thoughts of how I'm going to do this, how I am going to end the bullying.

Chapter Thirteen
Colomba-
A Grave
Warning

Walking away from the school bus to head to my house, I think about what I had asked Luis earlier. Was he telling me the truth when he said that he didn't know about anything wrong going on at our school? After what Nonna said and the creepy dream I had, I'm not really sure about anything anymore. Is something bad going to happen, or am I just going nuts seeing danger around every corner?

As I step into my house I am instantly greeted by Nonna who welcomes me with a warm hug.

"Hello Tesoro, how was school today?" a huge smile is on my face as I respond to her.

"I had a wonderful day, how was yours?" she smiles back at me as we both walk into the living room.

"Mine was pretty good too."

"Isn't someone going to ask me how my day was?" a voice says sarcastically. I look at the old leather arm chair in the corner of the room to see my dad with a book in his hand. I chuckle at my father.

"Of course, how was your day Dad?"

"Mine was pretty fantastic." my dad is a rather short man, but he is still a few inches taller than me. His dark brown hair is beginning to thin out on top of his head so that you can see his scalp. His bright blue eyes stare at me with intelligence and friendliness. My friends have told me that I don't look anything like my dad, but from pictures they have seen they all say that I look just like my mother.

"Well I'm glad." Nonna taps me on the shoulder as Dad returns to his book, when I look at her she silently ushers me into the kitchen where my dad can't hear us.

"What's up Nonna?" her eyes are full of concern, as if she thinks that the world is about to end.

"I don't know Tesoro," she closes her eyes, avoiding my gaze since she knows that she doesn't seem to be making any sense. "The feeling that something bad is about to happen is getting worse. I believe that from all of my time with that pin, I have grown a sense to detect when something is about to happen. If I am to believe what I feel, then something will happen within the next few days." I relax my tense shoulders.

"Nonna, I think everything is going to be alright. Maybe you are just nervous for me since I'm just starting high school. Everything seems fine at school, everyone seems so friendly, I don't think anything will happen." Nonna only shakes her head at me.

"Tesoro, when you have had this pin for a while you will start to feel things, you will start to sense when something bad is about to happen so that you can try to prevent it. You will need to learn to trust these feelings and not just ignore them like you are now with what I am feeling. Be careful, please promise me that you will." I still don't believe that there is any danger coming, but I can see that she is upset so I let myself give in to what she has to say.

"Alright Nonna, I promise that I will follow my instincts and protect anybody who is in danger." she smiles warmly, happy that I am taking her advice.

"That's my good girl, would you like to help me finish making dinner, we're having spaghetti with that garlic bread you love so much." I smile back at her, glad that the tension between us has disappeared.

As I help prepare the sauce for the spaghetti I think about what Nonna said about something bad happening. Will something actually happen sometime in the next few days? It doesn't really seem possible that something bad will happen, what I said to Nonna was true, everything seems great at school. Everybody is kind to me and I don't see anything bad happening to anyone else either, maybe something is happening when I am not around.

My mind thinks back on how Luis reacted when I said that I thought everyone was friendly at school, he seemed surprised and confused, as if he thought it was unbelievable for me to think that, as if I was lying. Is he going through some tough times at school? Is he in pain that I don't know about? Can I help him in some way to make his pain go away?

My heart aches to think that my friend might be sad and I haven't noticed. What kind of friend wouldn't notice when their friend is in pain? I must be a terrible, blind person to not see his pain. I shake my head to get that horrible thought out of my mind; I can't just assume things like that just because of one thing Luis said. He may have meant something else, he may not be miserable at all, he may be the happiest person in the world for all I know. As I add the last ingredients to the spaghetti sauce and stir them in with everything else, I think about everyone in the school that I know and try to figure out if any of them are suffering somehow and if I can somehow help them as Silver Dove. I want everyone to be just as happy as I am now. I can't stand the thought of anyone suffering when I am able to help them.

Chapter Fourteen
Luis-
My Bullies

First period is always horrible to make it through, it's one of the classes that I don't share with Colomba, and this is one class that I have with Alex. The teacher has her back turned to the class at the moment since she is writing on the board and a few people are definitely taking advantage of it. Alex uses this chance to lean over from his desk beside mine to take a handful of candy from the small bag on my desk and stuffing it in his mouth before I can stop him. When I look in the bag I can see that he took practically all of it.

I sigh, trying to ignore this as I take notes on what the teacher is saying, but I am interrupted by a piece of paper being thrown at the back of my head. Turning around, I find the piece of paper and pick it up. Looking at it, I can see that something is written on it in bright red letters. Opening the paper, I am greeted to only one word written in huge letters across the paper; "Loser".

I turn around again to see if I can find out who

did this, but I can't find any clue as to who threw this at me. I know that it wasn't Alex since he is beside me while this paper was thrown from behind. Behind me are several people that I knew in my old school who would pick on me, any one of them could have done it but I can't tell which one. I try to focus on my notes again, but my embarrassment makes it hard to think. Why do they pick on me even though I have never done anything to them?

I have never understood this; why do they pick on me? I've never really hurt anyone, I just sit quietly by myself most of the time. What made me so different from everyone else that singled me out for them to tease? I feel like crying as Alex starts poking me with his pencil, using the pointed side to poke my arm while a few other students behind him laugh. Why is this so funny to them? Why is him causing me pain so hilarious?

When the bell rings signaling the end of class, I quickly grab my stuff and rush out the door, leaving all of the people teasing me behind. I run down the halls heading toward my next class, only when I have made it to the classroom door do I slow down. I'm panting when I walk over to my desk, I can see that Colomba is already here. She is reading a book at her desk next to mine. When she sees me come into the room, she sets down her book and looks at me curiously.

"Hey Luis, why are you panting, did you run all the way here?" I smile at her awkwardly, knowing that I look ridiculous.

"Yeah, I... I wanted to get here as fast as possible, I didn't want to be late." she smiles at me.

"Well you succeeded, you're a few minutes early, most people don't show up until the last minute anyway." I feel my cheeks growing warm and I know that I'm blushing. I have a feeling that she knows that my excuse was fake, but I won't tell her the truth, that I was running to escape some people picking on me in my last class. I sit down beside her, still feeling like a complete idiot.

"How are you today Colomba?" I ask, trying to change the subject.

"I'm doing great, how about you?"

"I'm alright." Truthfully this morning hasn't been so bad compared to a lot of the mornings I have had to deal with my bullies. I'm just happy that she has had a good morning.

As we start talking about a new movie that's coming out soon that we both really want to see, another student comes in the classroom. I recognize him, his name is Ryan and he's one of the bullies I had back in middle school. He hasn't bugged me at all since high school started, but as he looks at me now, I have a feeling that these last few days of peace between the two of us is over. He sits in the desk behind me while Colomba and I continue talking. Even though I am enjoying the conversation, I still feel uncomfortable knowing that he's so close to me. I've always had these feelings that would tell me if something bad is about to happen, but ever since I got the Crow Medal these feelings have gotten stronger and they're usually always right. Right now, that feeling is going haywire, Ryan is definitely planning something.

The teacher comes in and starts class, I pay attention to the lesson while also keeping my eye on Ryan. I hope to catch him trying to do something to me so that maybe the teacher will see him doing it too and he will get in trouble for it and hopefully not do it again. I want to never have to worry about him doing anything to me again, especially since he is in this class with Colomba.

When class ends Colomba gives me a quick goodbye before she has to rush out the door since her next class is on the other side of the school and she only has a few minutes to get there. Ryan runs out only a moment after her, before he dashes out of the room though, he gives me a quick, evil grin that makes me realize that I didn't catch him, he did something while my back was turned. I reach down to grab my backpack to find that my bag is completely soaked. Bringing my hand back up I smell my wet hand, it has a very sweet smell, I can tell that it's soda. Ryan had purposefully spilled soda all over my backpack. Sighing under my breath, I pick up my bag and head to my next class, not even bothering to see what has been ruined in my bag. I'm only grateful that Colomba left before me and didn't see this. I would die of embarrassment if she did.

I open a door that leads into the stairwell. There are only two other people in the stairwell and they don't seem to notice that I am here with them. They are too busy having a very heated conversation.

"I don't understand, why are you breaking up with me if you know that the rumors aren't true?" A girl that I don't recognize is practically begging an unfamiliar boy as her eyes cloud over with tears. Her soon-to-be ex-boyfriend doesn't show her any mercy despite her crying.

"Didn't you see everything that they were putting on A-Streamer? They all were saying that you have been cheating on me, that you will go out with any guy even if you're dating me. I don't want to be seen with the girl that everyone talks about like that."

"But you know those rumors aren't true!" her voice echoes down the stairwell as her tears finally fall down her face and a feeble whimper leaves her lips. He looks in her eyes that are now red from her crying, but there is still no sign of compassion in his gaze.

"Who cares if they're not true?" he practically growls this terrible truth to her and she can no longer hold back her emotions. She sobs uncontrollably as he glares down at her. "I'm not going to be with a girl that everyone thinks is cheating on me, I'm not going to be the one that everyone pities because they think my girlfriend is going out with other guys behind my back. Just find someone else, apparently everyone else thinks that you can easily get another guy." After that last hateful comment, he turns away from her and only then realizes that they had not been alone.

"What are you looking at?!" he barks at me and I lower my gaze, a little frightened by his rage.

"Nothing, I didn't see anything." my voice is weak, and I know that he doesn't believe me, but he doesn't argue with me. He merely glares at me fiercely before he walks by me, ramming his shoulder into mine as he passes by, leaving behind his sobbing ex-girlfriend.

Cautiously stepping over to the crying girl, I rest my hand on her shoulder as her body is wracked with sobs.

"It will be alright, if that guy acts like this just because of some stupid rumors that he already knows aren't true, then you deserve to be with someone better. I know it hurts now, but it will get better." The girl stops crying for a moment to look up at me with venom in her eyes.

"How would you know; you don't understand anything about me?!" With that question hanging between us, she marches by me, using the back of her hand to wipe the tears from her face as her expression changes from one of deep pain, to deep hatred. With her gone, I am left alone in the stairwell. Hanging my head, I walk down the stairs and rejoin the giant mass of other students heading to their classes.

When I step in my next classroom, I slip off my bag and look inside to inspect the damage. Thankfully not much is wrecked, only a few soggy papers. Ryan must not have been able to spill an entire can of soda onto my bag, only a little bit, thank goodness.

I pull out all of the stuff I will need for class, trying to hold back my anger. Right now, I want to sneak into an empty room and bring Shadow to me so that she can transform me into the Crow and I can make Ryan regret what he did to me. I will make him so scared that he will never even think about teasing me again.

Sighing softly, I push that idea out of my head. I can't do something like that to Ryan just for dumping soda on my backpack, I just couldn't do something like that. I can't use my superpowers against someone just because they were mean to me, that would just be wrong. What Ryan did was wrong too, but I can't let that make me do the wrong thing. I want to be a good person, and I can't be a good person if I hurt people just because they do something rude to me. Everyone would probably think I'm a terrible person if I did something like that, and they would be right to do so.

The teacher walks into the classroom and starts the class. I take notes with my notebook smelling like a soda factory and my pencil sticking to my hand.

Chapter Fifteen
Colomba-
My Friends

Nat and I rush through the empty hallways, going to the library. We are both in study hall right now, so the teacher said that we could go and check out a book. Smiling joyfully, we start slowing down as we make it to the library doors. Slipping inside the silent room, we wander through the shelves, trying to find something interesting to read.

As we wander through the shelves, I notice somebody come through the door that I never would have expected to see in the library, Angela. She is holding her nose high in the air as she walks over to the librarian's desk, not even bothering to look at the books, and hands the librarian a stack of papers that she is holding.

"Here, my teacher told me to give this to you." Nat, the librarian, and I are all shocked by how rudely she said that, but none of us say anything about it, the librarian merely smiles at her.

"Thank you very much dear." Angela walks away from her without another word and heads to the door, eager to get out of the library as fast as possible. As she makes her way across the room, she sees me between the book shelves and she stops dead in her tracks, glaring at me.

"What are you looking at Colomba?" I want to say something mean to her, especially after she was so rude to the sweet librarian, but I will not return her rudeness. Instead I keep my anger in check and keep a straight face.

"Oh, I was just looking through the shelves to find something to read." she scoffs at me, smirking at me as if I am an idiot.

"I guess you have plenty of time to read Colomba, considering a person like you doesn't have much of a life." I know that she's only saying this to me because I stood up for Luis on the first day of school after he tripped over her purse. She tried to get him in trouble for it, but the principal, her father, couldn't really give him any kind of punishment for tripping over something and not causing any damage. Ever since then she has been very mean to me and Luis. I can take whatever Angela throws at me, I've been in school with her for years, I've gotten used to her, but Luis seems very sensitive. Every insult she throws at him seems to hurt him more than it does me. I just hope that he doesn't have to deal with her very much. I hold my head high as I stare right back at her.

"To you it may not seem like I have a life, but I'm happy and that's all that matters." she rolls her eyes at me and then storms out of the library. Nat comes around from behind the bookshelf beside me, looking from me, to the door that Angela just went through, and then back to me.

"What was all that about with Angela, she looked as if she was angry enough to throw a tantrum." I laugh.

"Yeah she's just been upset about what happened the first day of school with Luis." Nat looks surprised.

"Really? That seems like forever ago, and she's still mad about it? I think you have a new enemy Birdy." I pick a book off the shelf, smiling to myself.

"I think enemies are all that Angela has." Nat laughs at that as we both head to the library counter to check out our books. As Nat and I chat with the librarian, Mrs. Cobb, I think about what I said about Angela only having enemies, could she be the one that Nonna is so worried about, the one who might cause problems?

Angela is the kind of person who would do anything to get what she wants. Would she do something horrible if she knew that she could get something out of it? I push that thought out of my mind, I can't just start assuming that somebody is going to do something terrible without any evidence, that would just be wrong. Angela may not be a good person, but it doesn't mean that she's guilty of everything bad that goes on around here.

I smile as Nat and I head out of the library to go back to study hall. As we pass through the hallway the two of us laugh as Nat tells me about a story that one of her teachers told from his time in college. My mind wanders a bit as I wonder who could be the one who will cause the problems that my Nonna was talking about. I know that it couldn't possibly be Nat, she doesn't have a mean bone in her body, it might be Angela, but I kind of doubt it, and I don't think it would be Luis either, he's too nice of a guy to hurt someone else.

Why am I even thinking about this? I'm only thinking this because my Nonna had a funny feeling that something bad would happen, it doesn't mean that it actually will happen. I walk back into study hall, smiling joyfully with Nat beside me, both of us enjoying the peacefulness of this day.

Chapter Sixteen
Luis-
Training

In the back alley, behind my uncle's shop, I am in my form as the Crow, swinging my staff around to hit the targets that Shadow and I set up earlier. The targets are made of scraps of wood and metal that had been thrown away, not the best training equipment in the world, but it is functional and that's all that matters.

Over the past week, I have been training every night with my powers, improving in every way. I can now create the shadow creatures without any problem, I can fly really high and for a very long time, and I have also improved with my skills with this staff. Right now, I am practicing striking different parts of the target and no matter how fast I swing the staff I hit my target.

I am focusing on a target made of a few old planks of wood nailed together hanging from a branch of an oak tree by a rope. The target swings back and forth in front of me, my eyes lock in on it for only a second before I let my staff fly in front of me, striking the target dead in the center. I laugh as I let loose another flurry of strikes, each one hitting the target perfectly. The laugh fades from my lips when I realize something kind of important, I am hitting targets, but I am training so that I can one day fight against a person. I can't just hit targets, I need to imagine that these targets are people. If I don't start doing that now then I probably won't be able to do it down the road in real life.

As I stare at the target, I try to imagine a face on it. My mind flashes through the faces of many people that I know; I see the faces of some of my teachers, some people I share classes with, and some people that live near me, but I can't push myself to strike at any of them. All at once, a face flashes through my mind and then the intent stare that I was directing at the target is now a furious glare. In my mind, I am imagining the target as Alex. I can clearly see his smirking face on the target, he is laughing at me for not being able to strike the target while I was thinking about all of those other people, he thinks that I am weak. I release a roar of rage as I swing my staff, striking the target with so much force that it shatters, splinters of wood fly out and scatter across the concrete. All that remains of my target is a small piece of wood hanging limply from the rope that was holding it, which swings swiftly from side to side.

The image of Alex is destroyed, but I am not happy about it. Staring at the remainder of the target, I only feel shame. Did I really just do that because I imagined Alex's face on the target? That was kind of messed up. Am I really that messed up? I know that I have hated Alex for a long time because of everything that he has done to me, but would I really do something like that to him now that I have power?

Hanging my head, I let my form of the Crow fade so that I am now my normal self. Usually after practice I feel so much better than I did before, now I feel worse than I have for a long time. I walk up the back stairs to enter the upstairs apartment, left alone with my feelings of guilt.

Chapter Seventeen
Colomba-
Sword Training

I am in my dojo (or place where you study martial arts), class ended around half an hour ago, but my teacher and I are still training. My teacher, Jeff, has been training me for years and he is one of the greatest people I know. I have asked him if he could train me with swords after regular martial arts practice and he agreed without any questions. Jeff is an amazing martial artist, but his skill with swords exceeds everything else. With a sword in his hand, I bet that Jeff is unstoppable.

The dojo is one of my favorite places on earth, it is in a small building downtown and only has two rooms, the place where we practice martial arts and the back room where people get ready for practice. The room we practice in is very simply decorated; there are green mats all over the floor so that when someone falls during a technique it doesn't hurt as much, on the back wall there are three columns of racks where we keep the weapons that we practice with, and on the front wall of the room is a scroll with a single word in Japanese characters. I do not speak Japanese, but Jeff told me that it can be translated to interconnectedness, or to be connected to each other. He said that he wanted that word to be placed in the front of the dojo so everyone can remember that we are all in this together. No one is better than anybody else no matter how long they have been studying martial arts, we are all still learning, there is no end point.

We usually use katanas, or traditional Japanese swords, to practice in martial arts class, but I have asked Jeff to train me on how to use a sword like the one I have when I transform into Silver Dove. I didn't tell Jeff about my secret, I merely drew a picture of the kind of sword I have as Silver Dove and asked if he could train me with it. Apparently, it is called an arming sword or a knightly sword. Jeff explained a little bit about the weapon, it is a double-edged, straight blade sword and was used in the Middle Ages. It was used by knights in combat and I have to say that it is a pretty impressive weapon. Jeff and I have been swinging practice swords made out of wood at each other for quite a while and I am exhausted. It will take a lot of training for me to be good enough to use my sword as Silver Dove in combat.

Jeff keeps his sword at waist level and thrusts it toward me as he yells out, "Parry!"

Following his order, I quickly step back, getting out of the way of his strike and using my sword to block his thrust. He doesn't give me a second to rest before he gives me his next order, "Repost!"

Moving quickly toward him, I swing my sword

forward, aiming for his chest, but he easily blocks my attack and steps back a couple paces, holding his sword out in front of him, preparing himself for whatever I might do. Taking a deep breath, I strengthen my grip on my practice sword, gathering the courage to make the next attack.

I bring my sword above my head, intending to strike at Jeff's shoulder, but he lifts his sword as well and does a movement so quick that I can't even see it and my sword somehow flies out of my hand and clatters to the floor a couple yards away. Jeff holds his sword out in front of himself, pointing it directly at me. I hold my hands up in a surrendering gesture and he lowers his weapon immediately with a smile on his face.

"I think that's enough extra training for tonight, I believe your grandmother said that she was going to pick you up right about now anyway." I smile too as I nod my head. I don't want to stop practicing, but I know that I can't force him to stay here with me.

"Alright, thanks again for helping me with this Jeff, it means a lot."

"No problem Colomba, can I ask you something though?" I nod my head as I pick up my practice weapon.

"Sure, or course."

"Why did you want to learn how to use this weapon specifically?" he looks at me expectantly and I come up with a lie as quickly as I can.

"Well… I just wanted to learn something new and I always thought that those kinds of swords were pretty cool, so I wanted to try it." Jeff nods his head at me, completely satisfied with my answer. This is another reason why I like Jeff, he doesn't question you about stuff like this, he takes what you say by your word. He holds up his practice weapon, smiling at it.

"I haven't used one of these in a long time. I'm glad you asked to practice it with me." I wouldn't have believed that he hasn't practiced with this weapon in "a long time". By the expert way he was practicing with it earlier I would think that he has been practicing it every day for years.

"You're welcome, I hope that we can practice with it a bit more, I really enjoyed it."

"Of course, it will be nice to have someone to practice this with." In the backroom I can see Nonna entering through the back door.

"Well it's time for me to head out, I'll see you later Jeff." I wave goodbye as I take my practice weapons and head out the door with Nonna. Stepping into the car, I buckle myself in as Nonna starts the car and drives home.

"How was practice tonight Tesoro?" I release a deep breath, letting my body just melt into the seat, so grateful that I am staying still. I am completely worn out after training for so long with Jeff.

"Practice was fun, I really want to just take a shower and go to bed though." Nonna chuckles at me, not letting her eyes leave the road as she starts to leave town to head into the country, where our house is.

"Yeah, it looks as if you and Jeff worked very hard." I look down at myself to see that I am very disheveled. My martial arts uniform is wrinkled and hanging off of me, a few locks of hair have come out of the braid going down my back to hang in my face, and I am completely covered in sweat. I'm a bit glad that Nonna and Jeff were the only ones who have seen me like this, I look like I just survived a ship-wreck or something.

"How did it feel to handle the sword?" I think back on how it felt when Jeff first started showing me how to use the sword earlier. It felt strange to be using a different kind of sword than what I am used to using, but it also felt as if I have always known how to use it deep down, I just needed a little bit of a reminder. Maybe I felt that way because I am now the holder of the Dove Pin and that has somehow affected me, or maybe I'm just naturally good at this weapon, I'm not sure.

"It felt pretty great, but..." Nonna's smile falters when I say this.

"What is it Tesoro?"

"I- I don't know if I could ever use a sword on somebody. I love practicing with swords, I really do, but I don't think I could hurt somebody." Nonna nods her head, the smile no longer on her face.

"I understand, I felt the same way when I first became Silver Dove all those years ago. It is a hard thing to do, but you must remember that you have to do it to defend others, sometimes you need to do something you don't want to do so that you can help others."

The two of us fall silent as we both think about what she just said. I will have to hurt people if I am to become Silver Dove? I suppose every super hero in movies and comic books do, but nobody ever really mentions that fact, they just focus on all the cool things that the hero can do. I may just be hurting the bad guys, but I am still hurting someone, and I don't know if I can do something like that.

I have never really hurt anybody before, I've been studying martial arts for years, ever since I was just a little kid, but I have never used what I have learned to hurt somebody. I have always loved to learn martial arts, but I have never planned on using it to fight somebody. I always thought of it as something that I just enjoyed doing in the afternoon after school, now I am looking at it in a new light. Martial arts are about learning how to defend yourself, but in the hands of a cruel person, it can be used to hurt others.

My heart sinks to the bottom of my stomach as Nonna continues to drive. The city is now past us, only the forest surrounds the road now. It is a beautiful afternoon, but I hardly notice it at all. It is warm and full of life outside the car, but in my heart, there is nothing but ice. I am afraid of the powers I have been given when only a few hours ago I still felt excited about them. How can I bring myself to hurt someone even if they are trying to hurt me?

I can't think of an answer to that question as Nonna's car slowly makes its way through the forest while the two of us remain in silence.

<u>Chapter Eighteen</u>
Luis-
My Decision

As I pass through the halls of the school, I keep thinking about what Shadow asked me the other day; how do I plan on using my new powers to help the other kids like me, the bullied kids? Even though I have thought about it constantly since then, I still haven't come up with anything. How can I help the other kids like me if I can't even solve my own bully problems?

Colomba walks beside me with another one of her friends, Natalie. Natalie is telling Colomba all about this new book she has been reading while Colomba listens to her patiently, taking in every detail that Natalie says. Colomba and I just got out of our second period, Advanced Placement English, and even though we have shared that class for around three weeks I still feel so grateful that we both have it together. I still had to deal with Alex during first period but seeing Colomba right after almost made me feel better. I laugh with the two of them until the terrible moment when Colomba and

Natalie go down a different hallway and we part ways. The two of them give me a friendly farewell before they go into the classroom and leave me in the hallway, alone.

I pass through the halls to get to my next class, keeping my head down, hoping that none of my bullies will notice me. Walking quickly, I somehow remain unnoticed until I walk into my own class and sit down in my seat. The teacher walks in soon after me and starts the class. Nobody messes with me during class and I practically run out of the classroom to make sure that they don't catch me on the way out. I don't stop until I make it to the gym where Colomba will soon be coming out of. Ever since we became friends, I wait for her after class so that I can walk with her to her next classroom.

Leaning against a row of lockers, I wait for the gym door to open. Each second seems like hours whenever I am waiting for her, I'm just so anxious to see her smiling face again. Closing my eyes, I smile thinking about her, feeling completely at peace. Of course, that peace only lasts a moment before it is ruined.

"Hey there Louie." I open my eyes in terror at the voice of Alex. When I look over at him I can already see that it is too late to run away, he is only a few feet away from me, not even I could run that fast. He leans against the locker beside me, grinning at me evilly. "How you doin' today Louie?" I look away from him, not wanting to look him in the eyes.

"Fine." he chuckles at me, seeing my fear.

"Good, that's just great Louie. I was wondering if you could do me a favor. I don't seem to have any cash to go see a movie with some friends of mine later today and I was hoping you would be nice enough to give me a couple bucks." he leans in closer to me, I flinch away from him, which only makes his smile even bigger when he sees it. "Come on Louie, I'm sure you have something to help out an old friend like me." he places his hand on my shoulder, squeezing it tightly, making it obvious that his statement isn't a request, it's a demand.

I want to tell him no, that I don't have any money and even if I did, I wouldn't give it to him, but I'm afraid to, he's beaten me up for less. What could I say to him that wouldn't make him angry with me? I can't just give him all of my money. I work hard for every cent I have. I do little odd jobs around the neighborhood to earn what I have. I live right in the middle of the downtown area, in an apartment above my uncle's shop, so I usually help out with the other store owners to get a few bucks here and there; I won't let all of my hard work go to waste on someone like him. I feel a bit of bravery rise in me at that thought, but it doesn't last long when reality sinks in. If I stand up to him then he will just beat me up and take my money after school.

Alex stares down at me with that horrible grin on his face, waiting for me to say something, he seems amused by my discomfort, as if he can read my thoughts. My silent argument with myself is interrupted, even though I would usually be grateful when something interrupts Alex from harassing me, this time it is different, this time *someone* is interrupting.

"Hey Luis." turning around, I see Colomba walking over to me, a beautiful smile on her face. When Alex sees her, his eyes grow wide, surprised that such a pretty girl is talking to me. She stops in front of me, her perfect aquamarine eyes looking straight into mine. "Hey, I'm sorry for interrupting you guys," she looks over to Alex for a moment who is still staring at her with a stunned expression, "Hi Alex." I feel my heart stop for a moment, she knows Alex? Is he cruel to her as well as me, or does he plan to do what he always does with girls that he thinks are beautiful; flirt with them, date them, and then dump them? Alex wipes the surprised look off his face to smile at her confidently.

"Hey Colomba, how are you?" she smiles at him, and I feel my fists clench in rage.

"I'm alright, but I think I dropped my pen in our last class Luis, did you see anything, I need it for my next period." I smile back at her, trying to hide the embarrassment and pain that I had been feeling only moments before.

"No, I didn't see anything, but you can have one of my pens." I pull a pen out of my backpack and hand it to her. Her face lights up.

"Thank you so much Luis, you're a big help." the first bell rings and a bunch of students around us start running to their next class. "Well, I'll see you later guys, bye." she gives me a friendly wave as she turns around and walks down the hallway with Alex and I watching her as she goes. When she is no longer in sight, Alex grins an evil little smile.

"You have a really pretty friend Louie. I didn't

think that a girl like her would even bother to know your name, but I suppose she needs someone to get pens from every now and again." He chuckles darkly at his own joke while I feel myself trembling in anger. "I've been talking to her for quite a while in gym class and I have to say that she is one great girl." a shiver runs down my spine. "Maybe I should see if she's busy after school tomorrow. I would love it if she could cheer for me at the football game. What do you think Louie, do you think she would be interested in coming with me? I think that the two of us could have a pretty good time." he directs his evil smile at me, a deep hatred boils in my stomach.

"She would never be interested in you." Usually I would have never had the guts to say that to his face, but I can't let him near her. She may never go out with me, but I can never let her go out with him, he will never care about her. He just cares about how pretty she is, he doesn't care about her as a person. He doesn't care about how kind she is, how smart she is, or how selfless she is; all that matters to him is that she is beautiful. Alex only laughs at my courage.

"Well, let's just see what she has to say about that Louie." he walks away down the hall, laughing. As I watch him walk away, my anger just seems to grow and grow. I make my decision about how to deal with this in a second. I don't even give myself time to think it over before I have made up my mind.

Running into the boy's locker room, I thankfully find it empty. I open up my jacket and place my hand over the medal. Immediately Shadow appears in front of me, perched on top of one of the lockers.

"Hello Master, what can I do for you?" I smile at her, my anger disappearing as I think about what I am about to do.

"I have a problem Shadow that needs to be fixed and I think you can help me."

<u>Chapter Nineteen</u>
Colomba-
The First
Battle

The classroom is silent as we all work on a worksheet that the teacher handed out a few minutes ago. I hold the pen that Luis lent me, carefully answering each of the questions on the paper. For some reason this teacher only wants us to do our assignments in pen, seems kinda strange but I'm not going to argue against him. Everything is so quiet that I can practically hear the clock on the wall ticking, it's almost maddening how quiet it is in here. I'm kind of tempted to make a strange noise just to break the silence and make everyone laugh, but I resist the temptation since I know that it would annoy my teacher.

Nat sits beside me, diligently working on her assignment, I'm almost done with mine while she is only halfway through hers. As I finish writing a sentence, a strange feeling comes over me. The hairs on the back of my neck rise and a shiver runs down my spine. My mind immediately comes to the realization that something is about to happen, not something good either. Is this the feeling that Nonna told me about; the feeling that the pin would give me whenever danger is coming?

Glancing around the room I don't see anything unusual, everyone is just working on their paper, nothing else. My eyes pass by the window, but move back when I notice something, a dark shape, I can't really make out what it is. Staring at it intently, I notice that the shape is starting to get larger, squinting to try and see it better, my heart races when I can finally make out what it is. Grabbing Nat by her shirt, I pull her under her desk while I go under mine, the windows break apart, glass spreading all over the ground. The room that had been silent only moments before is now a chaotic storm of noise; students scream, desks topple over as people try to run away, and the strange shape growls furiously in the center of the room. It is only a few feet from me and I am too terrified to move away.

The creature is completely black, but it doesn't look as if it's solid, it's as if this creature is made of shadows. It looks like a massive, ferocious dog with coal black fur and burning red eyes. It looks like a demon in the form of an animal. The fur on the back of its neck is up as it lowers its head, growling furiously at everyone while they scream in terror. All of the students run out of the room while the demonic dog chases after them, leaving Nat and I alone in the classroom.

Only when it is out of sight do I crawl out from under my desk and hold out my hand to help Nat up.

"Are you okay Nat?" she nods her head as she breaths in deeply, her fear clearly shown in her wide eyes that dart to every corner of the room, searching for a new threat. "Alright, we need to-" I am interrupted by shouts of surprise and shrieks of horror that seem to echo throughout the entire school. Rushing to the classroom door, I glance outside to see that there isn't just one shadow creature, there are countless ones running after people or flying through the air, crashing through windows, tearing papers apart with their fangs, and knocking things over with their massive paws. What is going on?

"Colomba what are we gonna do?!" Nat bursts out anxiously as her entire body shakes, tears stream down her face. I wrap my arm around her shoulder and quickly lead her to the back of the classroom toward a large metal cabinet. Opening it up, I can see that it is practically empty, I usher Nat inside.

"Stay in here Nat and hide. I'll find another hiding spot since both of us can't fit in this cabinet. Just stay in here until everything is quiet, only then can you come out, not before. Everything will be alright, I promise."

"But Colomba-" I shush her, holding up my hand and she falls silent.

"Don't worry, I will be safe. I'll see you soon." before she can protest further, I close the door of the cabinet and run toward the window where I can see many more of the shadow creatures running around, chasing people. I need to find an empty broom closet or something so that I can transform into Silver Dove.

I need to stop these things somehow, but how? Where did these things even come from? What are they? If I don't know what they are, how can I defeat them? What am I going to do? As these thoughts rage through my mind, something disturbs my thoughts, something that I know will haunt me in my nightmares.

"Students of Drew's Hollow High!" a deep, menacing voice calls out and it suddenly feels as if I have just dived into a pool of ice water. I am actually trembling with fear.

I look around through the debris and strange shadow creatures flying around in the wind to see a guy dressed in a dark suit with a back mask covering his face, in one hand he holds what looks like a staff of some kind. The mask has a beak on it like a bird. What really catches my eye about this guy though is that on his back he has wings, wings with black feathers. With his dark wings, clothes, and that mask with the beak, he kind of looks like a giant, scary bird. I feel afraid as I stare at him.

He is flying high above everyone and everyone is staring up at him with the same mixture of fear and amazement. All of the students, as well as the shadow creatures, freeze in silence as we wait for this mysterious guy to continue speaking. I leap out of the broken window and step forward, completely amazed by what I am seeing. There is another person in Drew's Hollow with powers like me?

"Those of you who are being picked on and bullied, don't be afraid, but those of you who are the bullies, you *do* need to be afraid!" the other students begin to whisper amongst each other while I continue to stare in horror at the masked guy above us. "For those of you who have been bullying those who are weaker than yourself, I will find you and give you your just punishment." The guy in the mask chuckles coldly in pleasure, sending a shiver down my spine. "I am the Crow, and I am here to protect the weak!"

With that last word, the shadows start flying around again while all of the students below them run around in terror, screaming and crying out for help. A girl screams near me, I look to my left and see that one of the shadows is pulling on Angela's ponytail. Running over to her, I grab a math book that was lying on the ground beside an abandoned backpack and lift it high in the air, hitting the shadow with my book as hard as I can. The shadow flies off while Angela runs in the other direction, shrieking, not even bothering to thank me. I don't really care though. I look to my left to see that another shadow is pulling at Alex's jacket. I rush over to him as well to hit the shadow away, I run off as soon as the shadow is off of him so that I can run through the front doors of the school.

The shadows are flying all throughout the hallways as well, chasing after some of the students, while other students try to hide in lockers or classrooms. As one of the shadows flies by me, I quickly duck, running into an empty classroom as I pull out my cell phone, calling my Nonna, she answers on the second ring.

"Hello Colomba, is everything alright? You

shouldn't be calling from school."

"Nonna, you were right, something bad has happened. There is this crazy person with a bunch of shadow-like creatures that are tearing apart the school. What is going on?" she doesn't waste any time before she responds to me.

"What does this person look like, do they have wings like yours but black?" How did she know that?

"Yes, yes he does."

"Oh no," I hear her whisper into the phone.

"Why?! What's wrong?!"

"Colomba, listen to me very carefully. The person controlling the shadows is someone who has a pin similar to yours, it gives them powers as well. Their pin gives them the power to control those shadows as well as give other people superpowers. You must transform into Silver Dove, you have to defeat them, but you must not hurt them."

"What?! How can I defeat them if I don't fight them? Why can't I hurt them if they're trying to demolish the school?"

"Because, the only people who can wear those pins and receive superpowers are people with good hearts. There is a good person beneath the mask, you just need to convince them of that Colomba." My heart feels as if it is sinking in my chest. How am I supposed to do that? How can I convince this guy that what he's doing is wrong?

"Okay Nonna, I'll try."

"Good luck, Tesoro, I know you can do it." we both hang up, she may know that I can do it, but I certainly don't. Placing my hand over the pin, I take a deep breath and say that magic words.

"Peaceful warrior." I close my eyes as the pin begins to glow. When the light is no longer shining, I open my eyes to see that I am now Silver Dove. I take in a deep breath and let it out, getting rid of all my worry before I open the door back into the hallway and start flying through the air.

Those shadow creatures fly around me, they look surprised that something besides them is flying around. They all start rushing toward me, coming in to attack, but I don't let them get too close. Taking out my sword, I swipe it through the air at the closest one to me, the creature disappears completely. The others don't seem worried at all that their fellow shadow creature has been destroyed, they just keep coming toward me. I keep swinging my sword until all of the creatures around me have disappeared.

Flying through the halls, I take out any shadow creatures that I come across, until I make it to the front doors, I burst out of them and fly as fast as I can toward the guy who calls himself the Crow. When the Crow sees someone flying toward him, he doesn't move away from me, but I can see his body flinch in surprise. I stop about ten feet in front of him, the only sound between the two of us is the sound of our wings beating. After a minute or so, he breaks the silence.

"Who on earth are you?"

"I am Silver Dove, I am here to stop you." I say this calmly even though my heart is racing wildly, he glares at me from behind his mask.

"Why do you want to stop me? I am trying to

help all of the kids in this school who are getting picked on."

"You don't have to help them like this, there are other ways, you don't have to hurt the students."

"Those bullies need to pay for everything they have done to them, to me!"

"Sometimes the best revenge is just being happy. Don't obsess yourself over trying to punish them, focus on what you want in life and what you want to accomplish. Show them that they can't hurt you!" the fire in his eyes fades as he thinks about what I have said. The silence between us lasts for a few moments before the fire reignites in his eyes.

"No, they need to pay for what they have done to me!" All at once, a huge group of his shadow creatures suddenly fly at me, crashing into me like a ton of bricks. I fall to the ground while his shadow creatures pile on top of me, crushing me. From somewhere above me I can hear the Crow laughing at me, watching me fail.

Why did Nonna think I could do this? I haven't really done anything truly spectacular in my life. I'm only a kid, why would she give me a responsibility like this? As the shadow creatures keep piling on me, I can feel their weight crushing my armor, I think about giving up and surrendering, but one thought stops me from doing that, I think about my Nonna. She believes that I can do this, she must believe in me for a reason, no matter what I think about myself. I can't let her down.

Using all of the strength I have left, I kick my legs out, sending many of the shadow creatures flying into the air. As soon as those ones are off of me, it feels as if there is so much less pressure on me. I feel like I've been given more strength. I yank my arms out of the grip of the shadow creatures, taking my sword out of its sheathe. Swinging it through the air as fast as I can, I take out many of the creatures. My sword seems to fly as I keep swinging, my arms begin to tire out, but I don't stop swinging. I can't stop.

Through the mass of flying shadows, I see the Crow looking at me with a stunned expression as he watches me take down his shadow creatures. As soon as my sword cuts through a shadow creature it disappears like the shadow it is, only to be replaced by another shadow right after it. No matter how hard or fast I strike there are always more shadow creatures coming at me. Through all of the chaos I realize something; I can never defeat all of these creatures since the Crow will just keep making more of them while I get exhausted and then change back into my normal form, ending my super hero career as soon as it starts. To defeat the Crow, I need to face him one-on-one.

"Crow!" I manage to scream at him even though my lungs are hurting with each breath in my exhaustion. "Don't let these mindless shadow creatures fight your battles for you like a coward, fight me yourself if you think you can!" From this distance I can still see the Crow's hands clench into fists in anger at my words, completely stunned that I am challenging him directly.

After a moment of thought he raises his hand and all of his shadow creatures stop what they are doing and are frozen like statues. With a snap of his fingers the Crow's army of shadow creatures disappear to leave me and him alone in front of the school. He lands softly on the ground while I watch him carefully. My chest is heaving with each breath, I am worn out from my battle with the shadow creatures, but I still hold up my sword with what little strength I have left, pointing it at the Crow, trying not to show any of my fear to him.

I want to run away right now and hide with the rest of the students in the school. I want to throw down my sword and surrender. I want to not be the one standing up to this terrifying person, but I am. Looking at the Crow, I know that I need to be the one to stop him, nobody else has even dared to leave the school to fight back or even to say anything to the Crow. I have the power to do something good, so I need to be the one to protect them. Tightening my grip on my sword, I bring it up higher so that the blade is now pointed at his face. The Crow only glances down at my sword and chuckles.

"Do you really think that's necessary Silver Dove?" I glare at him behind my mask.

"Considering you were just having your shadow creatures attacking me, I'd say yes." He nods at that, understanding my point.

"We don't need to be fighting each other Silver Dove, we both have powers that have been given to us, we can actually make a difference in the lives of everybody in this school. We can help those who are being hurt by others, the kids who are bullied and teased every day. You and I can make sure that they are never hurt again." he tries to walk closer to me, but I bring my sword closer to him, making him stop. "You and I both know that there are mean people in this school who need to learn that they aren't invincible, that they aren't better than everyone else."

"There are people like that everywhere." I say, interrupting him. "We can't change all of the mean people in this world Crow, that's impossible." He nods his head.

"I know that Silver Dove, but it doesn't mean that we can't change our own little part of the world. We can make the school a better place and then move on from there, slowly we can make this world better."

"But you can't do it like this-"

"*Why not!?*" he screams, "Why can't I do it like this Silver Dove? You can clearly see that they are listening to me now! They may not have heard me before, but they hear me now! Whatever I say, they will do it, they know now what kind of power I have!" I swallow my fear as I say something that I know needs to be said but might anger him even more.

"You need to stop this, look how much pain you are causing everyone! Not just the bullies, but all of the students!" he looks around at the school to see that I am telling the truth. Many of the windows of the school are broken, papers are flying everywhere, and debris is scattered all over the place. Many of the students are cowering in fear, I can actually hear a few of them crying. The Crow sees this too, he can see the pain and misery he has caused. "If you keep this up you will cause everyone more suffering than any of the bullies in this school ever did! You can't fight their battles for them!" he turns his eyes away from me, but I can still see the pain that my words have caused him.

"You're right." He looks back up at me, sadness in his tone. "I made a terrible decision today." He looks around at the students with a thoughtful look. "I can't fight their battles, but I can help them fight their own battles. Good bye Silver Dove, we will meet again."

"*Wait* what do you mean by that!?" He doesn't answer me. All of his shadow creatures reappear and start flying around him at an incredibly fast pace until they are all nothing but a dark blur. All at once the darkness fades and there is nothing left of the Crow or his shadows. I look around, but I can't see him anywhere, he is gone.

What did he mean by that last remark? What does he mean that he's going to help the bullied kids fight their own battles? How could he possibly help them with that? I close my eyes as I push that thought out of my mind. There is no way that I can figure out what he meant. I can't understand someone like him who would think that attacking the school is a good idea. Instead of thinking about that, I focus on what is happening right now. Right now, there are many people in this school, students and teachers, who are afraid, and they don't know what's going on. They are the ones that I need to help. I swallow back my apprehension as I clear my throat and yell out loud enough for everyone to hear me.

"Everyone don't be afraid; the Crow is no longer

here!" A few fearful faces appear at the broken windows and through the doorways to listen to me. I actually see Nat's face appear from the window of the classroom I left her in. My entire body feels weightless with joy when I see that she wasn't injured in all of this. "I am Silver Dove, I am here to protect all of you! No matter what will happen, I will try my best to keep all of you safe! No matter what, I will stop whoever means to hurt you because I am a warrior of peace, and I will bring peace to this school again!" Just like how my Nonna taught me, I place my hand over the dove emblem on my armor and say the magic words. "Bring peace little dove."

At the sound of my words, the dove on my armor flies off of my chest and flies high into the air. When it is far above the school, the silver of its feathers shines brightly in the sunlight, it glows brighter and brighter until I have to close my eyes to keep them from hurting. When the light has faded, I open my eyes to see that the school is fixed; the windows are no longer broken, there isn't any junk flying around, and there is no sign of the destruction caused by the Crow at all. When all of the students see what has happened, they begin to cheer, running out of the school toward me. They all want to embrace me, to shake my hand, and thank me, but I do not need their praise. I fly high into the air before any of them can reach me, as they all gather beneath me, I wave down at them and smile.

"If anything like this should happen again, I will be there to help, I promise!" They cheer for me as I fly off into the distance, getting away before any of the teachers or the principal can stop me to ask questions. Over the intercom, I hear the principal announcing that school will end early for the day considering everything that just happened. I smile as I fly into a bunch of trees and transform back into my regular self before I return to the school to find Nat. It doesn't take long to find her and we both impatiently wait for the bus while we talk about what happened, but I am more eager to tell Nonna everything that has happened today.

Chapter Twenty
Luis-
Shadow Explains,
I Ignore

I run into my room, slamming my door behind me in rage. I just got through calming down my Uncle Diego. He had heard about everything that happened at school today and he was afraid that I might have gotten hurt. It took me almost twenty minutes to calm him, he seemed so angry that the Crow was scaring everyone. First, he asked me a bunch of questions, wondering if everything he had heard about the Crow having magical powers was true. Then, he started a tirade about how horrible the Crow must be. I tried to tell him that the Crow (*me*) was only doing all of that to defend all the bullied kids, to help people, but he said that the Crow was nothing more than someone using their abilities to scare people, that the Crow was the real bully in this situation. I can't believe he said that about me! I know that he doesn't know that it was me doing all of that stuff, but it was still painful to listen to.

With the door closed firmly behind me, I feel safe enough to place my hand over my pin and Shadow appears on my dresser, looking down at me with sorrow in her dark eyes.

"Hello Master." she greets me with a soft voice.

"Hey Shadow, what happened today? Why did that girl, Silver Dove, stop me? I was doing the right thing, I was trying to stop the bullies from hurting anybody else." Shadow narrows her eyes at me skeptically.

"Are you sure that's the only reason why you chose to come out as the Crow at that moment? I saw that Alex was going to try to ask Colomba on a date right before you called me. Do you think that this might have helped you make your decision about when to reveal yourself?" I glare at Shadow.

"That had nothing to do with it Shadow. I'm doing this to help the other bullied kids. It was only a coincidence that that happened today, Colomba had nothing to do with my decision! I'm going to help bullied kids like me!" Shadow doesn't really look like she believes me, but she apparently decides to let it go and move on with the conversation.

"Yes, your heart was in the right place, but you didn't do it in the best way." I narrow my eyes at her.

"I don't understand." Shadow flies off my dresser to rest on my arm.

"You tried to stop people from hurting others by hurting them. Sometimes giving people a taste of their own medicine isn't the best thing to do." I glare at her, shaking her off my arm so that she flies off my arm and onto my bed.

"You sound just like Silver Dove." She looks at me with a steady, uncomfortable stare.

"Is that such a bad thing Master?" My fists clench in rage.

"You don't understand me either, I thought you, out of everyone, would understand me, but you're just like everybody else! You think I'm a horrible person for doing this, but I'm doing this to help people! I want to end the pain of everyone like me, the kids who feel afraid to go to school every day since they know that they will get hurt by some of the other kids at school! The kids who get picked on for things that they can't control! The kids who need someone to help them because no one else will! I will be that someone for these kids, I will help them with these powers you gave me!" Shadow shakes her head slowly, closing her eyes in her sadness.

"Master, you can't fight these battles for them-"

"That's just it though Shadow, I will use my powers so that all the bullied kids will be able to stand up for themselves. I will make sure that none of them will be picked on again." Shadow stares at me, completely confused.

"I- I don't understand Master, how do you plan on doing this?" I chuckle, thinking about how Silver Dove won't be able to stop me from completing my mission. She may be powerful, but she has no power over me.

"Don't worry Shadow, you'll find out soon enough." I stare out my window to the street below, watching cars pass by. As I think about my plan I chuckle softly, finally feeling excited about going to school tomorrow, knowing that tomorrow is where my plan begins.

Chapter Twenty- One
Colomba-
The Crow's
Medal

"Nonna! Dad! Is anybody home!?" I yell out as I walk through the front door of my home. I am not greeted by an acknowledgement, but instead by a set of welcoming arms that embrace me tightly.

"Tesoro, I am so proud of you!" Nonna is practically crying in her joy as she says this to me. "I saw everything that happened." She releases me from her hug while I stare at her, completely confused.

"What do you mean you "saw everything"? Were you at the school?" She shakes her head at me, the smile still present on her face.

"No, you need to come see this." She leads me over to the living room, where the local news is playing on the television. A news anchor stares out from the television at me with unemotional eyes.

"This amateur video was taken by a student at the scene of the incredible fight earlier today at Drew's Hollow High School." The news anchor disappears from the screen to be replaced by a video of me as Silver Dove flying in front of the Crow. I can't hear what is being said by the two of us, but the Crow looks very angry as he screams at me and suddenly a bunch of his shadow creatures appear and attack me while I fight them off with my sword. My sword slices through countless shadow creatures and they disappear into thin air.

My hands clench into fists at the sight of the battle. I can still feel my hands around my sword, cutting through the monsters so quickly that I barely even saw my sword as it would pass in front of me. I am exhausted just thinking about that battle, in my excitement I only realize now how tired I really am. The video ends abruptly so that the camera can return to the news anchor.

"Although there are no details at the moment as to the identity of these two teenagers, only one thing is for certain, this will not be the last time we see them." The news anchor ends that last sentence very dramatically before they turn their attention to the weather man. Nonna picks up the remote and turns off the television, no longer interested in what they have to say. Even though the television is off, I still stare at it, gazing at it in wonder.

"Wow, I- I don't know what to say. What are we going to do about all of this? Who was that guy at school anyway?" Nonna's smile disappears in an instant.

"That person is known as the Crow, they create and control those shadow creatures that attacked your school, they also have the power to give other people super powers. Their powers, like yours, come from an object that they wear, a medal. It is said that the person who wears the Crow Medal is supposed to be a partner to Silver Dove, assisting you in helping create a more peaceful world." Nonna shakes her head in disappointment. "Apparently this Crow seems to have different plans for the medal."

Nonna looks over at an old photograph of her and my grandfather when they were teenagers back in Italy, before they immigrated here after the war. In the picture, my grandfather is holding onto my grandmother as they both smile at the camera, the two of them sitting on top of a picnic blanket on the banks of the Tiber river in Rome.

"Your grandfather was the one who wore the Crow Medal before this. It was lost years ago, and we thought that we would never see it again. It's funny that I get to see it now in my old age." She chuckles, her eyes clouded by sadness as she reminisces of the days when my grandfather was still alive. He passed away when I was ten, so it has been a long time since he passed away, but the pain is still fresh in the heart of my Nonna and me.

"When I received the Silver Dove Pin I was working as a secretary for a general during WW2, while your grandfather was working making ammunition for the resistance fighters who tried to go against the Nazis and the Italians who were loyal to their cause. They would not allow your grandfather to fight with them since he was small and weak in their eyes. They felt that he would die on his first mission if they let him join their crusade. We used our abilities to fight against the Nazis stationed in Italy in secret so that Hitler and his followers wouldn't try to catch us to find the secrets of our powers." I stare at her with unhidden surprise. My Nonna is super freaking awesome! I've always known that, but I didn't know she was awesome to this extreme. How on earth can I, as Silver Dove, live up to a legacy like that? I don't think it's possible!

A sudden thought occurs to me and the words leave my mouth before I can find a more delicate way of asking it. "You said that to have the Medal give you superpowers, you have to have a good heart. If this guy has a good heart then why were they wrecking everything at the school?" she smiles at me, the sadness still present in her eyes.

"Sometimes good people do bad things because they feel as if they are doing it for the right reasons." I shake my head at her, confused by her words.

"You lost me." Nonna rests her hand on top of mine, she waits a moment before she speaks, unsure of how to explain this to me.

"There are many good people in the world, but some of them don't know how to do the right thing in the right way. They can have wonderful motivations, but they don't know how to reach those goals without hurting others. They can be trying to help some people, but they may hurt someone else to get there. They may not mean to hurt others, but it happens, and they have to live with the consequences." She shakes her head in disappointment. "I can't believe that Shadow would let all of this happen, I would think that she would choose her master more carefully." I look at her, more confused than ever.

"Who's Shadow?"

"Shadow is the guide for whoever wears the Crow Medal. Since the Crow has a very dangerous power to give other people super powers and has stronger abilities than yours, Shadow was created to help whoever has the medal stay true to their path. Shadow is the servant of whoever wears the medal, so she can't tell whoever wears the medal what to do, but she can provide advice and wisdom so that the Crow can make the best decision possible when using his powers. I suppose that Shadow has failed with this one though, at least for the moment." I look down at my hands, not wanting to say what is on my mind, but I know that I need to tell her.

"I was really scared today, I thought that I couldn't beat him. He's so strong compared to me." Nonna nods her head, looking a little sad.

"Yes, the powers of the Crow are actually stronger than yours, but that doesn't mean that he will win in the end. You just have to be smarter than him. He may be strong, but you are a very intelligent girl, I've seen you outsmart people twice your age, if you can do that then you can outsmart the Crow. If this Crow does have a good heart buried within him, then you will just have to show him the right path, to help him use his powers for good." I feel my heart sink at her words.

"Yeah, well I don't think that that will happen for a really long time, you should have heard the Crow at school. He believed that he was doing the right thing by sending all of those shadow creatures around the school, terrorizing everyone. How can I make someone like that change their mind?" Nonna shrugs her shoulders.

"I'm not sure, maybe it will come with time. He will probably try many things to do what he thinks is right and you will defeat him a few times, and maybe after a while he will come to see that you are not his enemy and are here to help him create a more peaceful world. We just need to wait for him to come to his right senses." I smile at her, hope rising in me again.

"I think you're right. This is probably going to be a very long wait though." Nonna chuckles at my remark.

"I wouldn't doubt it, from the way you described this young man, he seems very stubborn. Now let's stop talking about this depressing topic and let's start making dinner. Your father will be home soon from work and I promised to make him grilled chicken and an apple pie for dessert." I grin joyfully, letting the memory of what happened today fade from my mind to focus on the present.

"I'll make the pie if you make the chicken." She holds out her hand to me and we shake hands.

"It's a deal Tesoro." We both walk into the kitchen, the dark subject of the Crow forgotten as we focus on making a delicious dinner.

<u>Chapter Twenty- Two</u>
Luis-
Lies on the
News

I storm into my room, no longer able to control my anger. Uncle Diego and I just finished dinner and he spent the entire time talking about what I did at school today. Condemning the Crow for sending the shadow creatures around the school and praising Silver Dove as if she is some kind of angel protecting the school against a horrible demon. I'm surprised that I was able to keep a straight face while he was unknowingly insulting me. Now that I am alone in my room, I move my hand to place it over the medal to bring Shadow to me, but I change my mind. She's probably just going to repeat exactly what my uncle said, that I shouldn't have done it, blah, blah, blah.

Instead of doing that, I pick up the TV remote and turn it on. The local news is the first thing that appears when it turns on and my eyes open wide when I see something familiar on the corner of the screen, it is a picture of me as the Crow and Silver

Dove. I listen intently to the news anchor as she talks with a completely expressionless face despite the strange story she is telling.

"Only four hours ago, the tranquility of the small town of Drew's Hollow was shattered as something unbelievable happened in their local high school, two super powered teenagers fought in the air and then disappeared without a trace. At approximately two o'clock this afternoon, a teenage boy, dressed in an all black costume and with black wings coming out of their back, who referred to himself as the Crow, created strange creatures that terrorized the entire school. This mysterious young man stated, according to eye-witness reports, that he was the protector for the weak, that he was going to use his powers to protect the bullied children of the school and give the bullies their "just punishment". It was then that another superpowered teenager entered the picture, a young woman in armor with white wings coming out of her back, who referred to herself as Silver Dove. This brave young lady apparently tried to reason with the Crow, to make him stop attacking the school, but the Crow merely sent all of his monsters to attack her instead. Silver Dove then fought off all of the monsters and then battled with the Crow before he disappeared among a crowd of his creatures."

So, the people on the news think that I did the wrong thing too. Great, now they're going to make everyone think that I'm the bad guy even though I'm trying to help people. The news anchor continues talking about this story while my hands clench into fists of rage.

"After the Crow disappeared, Silver Dove announced to the entire school that she was devoting herself to protecting them from whatever threat will come." Oh, so Silver Dove is telling people that she's going to protect them too? She thinks that she will be able to solve everyone's problems, but I bet she doesn't even realize just how terrible it is to go to school every day for some people. I bet that she thinks that she just needs to protect everyone from me, but she doesn't realize that the threat is coming from inside the school, it comes from all of those kids who pick on people like me just because we are a little bit different from them! *Silver Dove doesn't understand anything at all!* I glare at the screen, almost daring the news anchor to say anything else good about Silver Dove.

"After that Silver Dove used her abilities to fix all of the damage caused by the fight between her and the Crow." Okay, didn't think she would be able to do that. I guess it's nice to know that I won't be going to school tomorrow in what looks like a bomb sight. A super power like that could come in handy. I kind of wish I could have a power like that. Actually, I wish I could have some of her powers, she definitely had super strength and she can fly a lot faster than me. I suppose I'm a bit jealous of what she can do; with my powers I have to rely on my shadow creatures to get what I want done while she can take care of things herself.

"No one is quite sure how this all came about, or why, but it is quite obvious that this won't be the last time we see Silver Dove and the Crow."

I chuckle at what the news anchor says while I

growl at the television, "That's the only thing you've gotten right so far." I click a button on the remote and the TV turns off. I toss the remote onto my desk before I fall back onto my bed, closing my eyes, trying to forget about what happened, at least for the moment. I don't realize it, but as I lay down I accidently rest my hand on top of the Crow Medal and Shadow appears on my dresser.

"Good evening Master." Her voice is dark, as if she really doesn't want to wish me a "good" evening. I almost fall off my bed in surprise when I hear her voice.

"Oh, hello Shadow." I don't bother to hide the dark tone of my voice either. It's clear that neither of us really want to talk with each other. As I look at her I want to hide, I don't want to see the anger in her black eyes. "I suppose you can guess what everyone is saying about what happened at school today."

"Of course, I already know everything," her voice seems to cut me like a razor, "when you cannot see me I am still here. I see *everything* that you do. I don't even think I need to say this since you probably know, but I am disappointed in you Master." I look up at her, completely surprised.

"You're disappointed in me?" I scoff at her, feeling disappointed in her. "I was trying to help people and then Silver Dove comes around and ruins everything. She tells everyone that she is there to help them even though she stopped me from helping them."

"You weren't helping Master, you were hurting." She flies off my dresser to land on my knee. "Silver Dove is meant to be your ally, not your enemy. She has the right idea about how to use her powers, stopping those who are trying to hurt people, at the moment, that means you." Her dark eyes narrow at me with contempt. In my anger, I shake my knee so that she has to fly off my knee to land on my bed.

"Shut up Shadow, I don't need to hear this from you! I'm your master so I don't want you to say any more about what you think about Silver Dove." I immediately regret what I said, Shadow has shown me nothing but kindness, yet I yell at her. What is wrong with me?

"I'm sorry Shadow, I'm just angry about all this." I look out the window, "I just wish that I could talk to her, make her see that I'm not her enemy."

"Well.... you can." She sounds hesitant, as if she doesn't want to explain.

"What do you mean Shadow?"

"Well... you..." I glare at her, feeling all of the insults that the news has been directing at me, building a deep rage in my heart.

"Shadow I am your master, you have to tell me if I am able to talk to Silver Dove or not." Shadow lowers her head, her thin beak releasing a defeated sigh.

"Yes, you can talk with Silver Dove. Since your pins are controlled by the same magic, you two are connected so you can send a message to her as long as she is wearing the pin. You can speak with her, but you cannot see her. No matter how far you two are apart, you can still speak to each other. To send her the message you must place your hand over the medal and say, "Speak to Silver Dove." and it will open up her mind to your words." Shadow ends her explanation and still doesn't look at me. I believe that she's angry at herself for having to reveal that to me. I don't say anything to her in reply, instead I place my hand over the medal and say four simple words that creates a block of ice in my stomach.

"Speak to Silver Dove."

Chapter Twenty- Three
Colomba-
The Voice

Looking out my bedroom window at the night sky, the stars are shining down on me, completely peaceful. As if they didn't even notice the massive fight that happened beneath them earlier this afternoon. I still can't believe that this happened to me, it almost feels like it was a dream. Who could believe that they turned into a superhero and fought a super villain at their school and saved the day? Nobody would really think that something like that could happen in real life. It could easily happen in the movies or in comic books, but not real life. If you told somebody about this who didn't witness what happened, they would think that you are crazy.

I think I'm a little crazy right now thinking about what happened. I don't know what to think about all of this, all I know is that I am both proud and scared. I'm proud that I fought someone who was trying to hurt many of the people in my school, yet I am also scared because I have a feeling that the Crow isn't done with me. He still has something planned to accomplish what he failed to do today.

Closing my eyes, I take in a deep breath and try to empty these strange thoughts from my mind. I need to relax so that I can get some sleep. After all that happened today, Nonna wants to spend more time training me on how to use my super powers and I can't say that I blame her. I want to train more too so that I can be prepared for the next time the Crow decides to show his masked face again. I try to find some peace in the quiet of the night, but the silence is disturbed by a frightening voice that chills the blood in my veins.

Silver Dove. I turn around so quickly that I hear my back pop, but there is no one behind me. Silver Dove. Only now do I recognize the voice, it is the voice of the Crow and he is speaking to me, but he's not here, it's like I'm talking to a ghost.

"Crow?"

Yes, it is me Silver Dove, you and I had a very interesting fight today. I was hoping that you would see that I am doing the right thing, but I was mistaken, you didn't see sense.

"No Crow, you are the one not seeing sense. You can't hurt these people just because they have hurt you-"

I am teaching them a lesson!

"*No! You're just getting revenge!*" I calm myself down so I can try reasoning with him. "You are a good person, deep down, if you weren't your medal wouldn't have worked for you. Please, just see that hurting them isn't the right thing to do. Even if they are mean people it doesn't mean that you have to be mean to them." I hear him chuckle at me in my mind.

You are so stupid Silver Dove. Those people, those bullies, need to learn their lesson or else things will never change. I close my eyes and take in a deep breath to swallow back my pride as I reveal something to him.

"Crow, you aren't alone in this, when I was little, in third grade, I was picked on constantly. One of the other kids spread rumors about me, telling everyone that I picked my nose, that I wet the bed, and that I still slept with my baby blanket, anything to humiliate me. Many of the other kids stopped playing with me because of those rumors, all except one person, my best friend. She stayed beside me no matter what everyone else said about her. She knew that what the other kids said didn't matter because I was her true friend and if the situation was reversed I would not have abandoned her."

I remember all of that clearly, it was a very dark time in my young life. Angela was the one who spread the rumors about me. I believe she was just upset that many of the kids didn't want to play with her because she was unkind to them while I never had trouble finding someone to play with me. After she spread those rumors though many of my playmates disappeared, all except Nat of course. She stayed beside me, never letting her loyalty waiver, she acted as if the rumors being spread about me didn't even exist and, eventually, they did end up disappearing and all of my old playmates returned to join us. She stayed with me, never even complaining about how the other kids ignored the two of us. For that I will always consider her to be my best friend. The Crow is silent in my mind, I can only hope that he's silent because he is thinking about what I have said. As the silence hangs between us I decide to keep going with what I feel needs to be said.

"You need to stop thinking about what others say about you and focus on who really matters in your life. Those are the people you need to listen to since they want what is best for you." I feel myself shiver in fear and anticipation for what I am about to say. "I can be that friend for you. If you need someone to lean on, I will be there if you want. I can help you." Silence follows my offer and I stand alone in my room, anxiously waiting for his response. An eternity seems to pass before he finally says something.

I don't want to be friends with someone who wants to stand in the way of what needs to be done. With my plan in action things will change, if I follow your advice then all of those horrible people in this school will win. Thanks for the offer, but I'm not interested in your friendship. Good night Silver Dove, we will see each other again soon. And with that said he is gone. I can no longer feel his presence in my room, I am, once again, alone.

I take a deep breath as I sit down on my bed, closing my eyes as I try to calm myself. I was so terrified hearing him speak to me in my own room, it's almost as if he can be anywhere. That thought sends a shiver of fear down my spine. Before I do anything else, I get up off my bed and search my room just to make sure he isn't in here with me. I know that it's silly, but I need to make sure that I am alone. Only when I am completely sure that nobody else is with me do I sit back down on my bed.

Looking outside at the dark, moonless night, I wonder about what has happened in the Crow's life to make him so angry, to make him think that this is the right path to take. I have been picked on many times in my life, but I haven't let that control my life, I moved on from my pain, but it looks like the Crow hasn't.

"Good night Crow," I say this out loud to the night outside. "I hope that, wherever you are, you are happy, and that we can find a way to solve all of this. I don't want to fight someone who is in as much pain as you."

I turn out my lights and crawl under my covers, getting ready for bed. As my eyes close, I know that when I get up in the morning I will have to be observant, I will have to try and find the Crow. I need to make sure that he doesn't hurt anyone like he tried to do today because I know he wasn't lying to me, I will see him soon.

Eliza Scalia is currently a Masters student for Clinical Mental Health at Troy University. She enjoys reading and needlework, as well as hanging out with her two pets, her dog Maggie and her cat Dusty. Eliza has been writing for many years and has self- published the Death's Assistant series for young adults.

www.ingramcontent.com/pod-product-compliance
Lightning Source LLC
Chambersburg PA
CBHW070511200726
48293CB00007B/2482